# Money-Makin'
# Mamas 2

# Money-Makin' Mamas 2

*Silk Smooth*

*www.urbanbooks.net*

Urban Books, LLC
97 N18th Street
Wyandanch, NY 11798

ISBN 13: 978-1-62286-782-0
ISBN 10: 1-62286-782-3

First Trade Paperback Printing December 2016
Printed in the United States of America

10 9 8 7 6 5 4 3 2 1

Distributed by Kensington Publishing Corp.
Submit orders to:
Customer Service
400 Hahn Road
Westminster, MD 21157-4627
Phone: 1-800-733-3000
Fax: 1-800-659-2436

# *TAFFY*

## 1

This life of mine was a motherfucker, and I had my three daughters, Chyna, Simone, and Karrine, to thank for that. I felt that something had gone horribly wrong, and when the phone kept ringing, it confirmed my suspicions. Honey didn't just call me back-to-back, unless it was important. I was on my way home from a friend's house—yeah, that's right . . . I had to get my fuck on every now and then too. Just because I was fifty-two didn't mean my pussy had dried up and couldn't be put to use. But you had better believe that the fine motherfucking nigga I had been giving all this good pussy to was worth it.

"What's going on, Honey?" I asked with an attitude. You would think that after getting some good dick I would be happy, but the thoughts of my daughters always consumed my mind.

"We got a problem."

"Okay. So handle it. I'm tired and I'm on my way home. Must you call to bug me about every goddamn little thing?"

"It must be that time of the month for you. Then again, I suspect that you don't have periods anymore, so why you sounding shitty?"

This nigga was tripping. I didn't have time for small talk, so I hung up on his ass. When he called back, I didn't bother to answer. I kept it moving to the crib, but ten minutes away from home, I did a U-turn in the middle of the street and headed to Honey's house because I had a gut feeling that something wasn't right.

By the time I got to Honey's house, it was almost one o'clock in the morning. I used my key to let myself in, but as soon as I entered I heard someone screaming out. The screams were more like a moan and a cry, and were starting to work my nerves.

I took a few steps forward and could see a light-bright bitch straddling the top of Honey while he lay back on the couch. Her backside was facing me and her long, coal-black, curly hair fell far down her back. Honey had a tight grip on her ass that looked like it could use a little Botox to clear the wrinkles. From the way she was hollering, he was definitely putting something on her.

"I love this big black dick," she shouted while bouncing up and down on him. "Yo . . . you make my pussy feel so good, Honey. Damn it feels *good!*"

At least she was satisfied, but Honey couldn't have been. The bitch was moving more of her back than anything. She damn sure didn't know how to grind her pussy. If I'd had my gun, I would have shot her ass dead for disappointing my son. And the sad thing was that she appeared to be a beautiful white woman. But everything that looked good wasn't always good to you.

While leaning against a thick column in the foyer, and getting a thrill out of watching this bullshit, I lit a cigarette and started to smoke. The lighting in the room was dim and a few candles were lit, I guess to set the mood. I hadn't heard Honey grunt not one damn time. I was five seconds away from going into the room to break this heifer off with some sexual tips or something.

"Get up and turn around," Honey said, opting for another position.

The chick didn't hesitate to turn around with her ass now facing him. She carefully eased down on his dick that was standing tall like a black stick, hard as ever. I was kind of shocked by how big he was. No wonder Karrine had been tripping.

Unable to handle him, the chick cried out again. I mean fuck all the screaming and hollering, moaning and groaning bullshit . . . put in some work and make his ass holler too! I was getting frustrated watching this mess and had taken a long drag from the cigarette then whistled smoke into the air.

"Pu . . . put your fingers in my ass," she shouted. "Fucking play with my clit and then I'll cum all over your face so you can suck cum from my pussy!"

Hell fucking naw. Did she really just say that dumb shit? She was expecting him to do all of that with her *tiddays* bouncing around and her pussy not doing nothing? As she bent over to display her ass to him, I guess he honored her wishes because she kept gasping for air and humming. I just didn't understand young people these days. This unnecessary, freaky shit was too much.

I dropped the cigarette on the marble floor then smashed it with the tip of my pointed stiletto. This was a waste of time. As the bitch sat on top of him backward with her eyes closed and mouth wide open, I walked further into the great room. While holding the chick's hips and pumping his dick into her, Honey quickly raised up when he saw me. His quick move caused the chick to open her eyes.

"Who the fuck are you?" she barked, then turned her head around to look at Honey. He was speechless at first, but he patted her ass and ordered her to get up.

The bitch had the nerve to ask why. Was the dick that good that she couldn't jump off of it?

I folded my arms and my whole face twisted. "Why? Because I'm his mother, that's why. Have some damn respect and get yo' ass up. You wasn't doing anything no goddamn way."

Honey knew this was about to turn ugly, so he sat up, causing her to rise up too.

"Go upstairs to the bedroom all the way at the end of the hall," he said to her. "I'll be there shortly."

There was a look of embarrassment on the chick's face. I couldn't help but to fuck with her.

"Why do some of y'all chicks always go for the black dick and don't know what to do with it? I don't get it. If y'all can't handle it, just leave it alone."

Her eyes bugged. She tried to catch an attitude. "I couldn't care less that Honey's a black man. And have you ever had to sit on anything like that before? Trust me, it ain't easy."

She had a point about that, because Honey was, indeed, packing. Ray certainly didn't have it like he did.

"If you couldn't care less that he's a black man, then you need not specify the color of his dick when he's fucking you. Furthermore, gon' and take yo' ass upstairs like he told you to. I don't appreciate the tone you've taken with me, and must I remind you again that I am his mother."

She walked her trashy ass away and headed upstairs. By then, Honey had sat up on the couch and was in the process of lighting a joint.

"I called to tell you that we had a problem," he said nonchalantly. "But you hung up on me."

"So? What you gon' do about it? Cry? In case you haven't recognized me, I'm here. I came to see what was up, didn't I?"

Honey sucked in heat from the joint, then reached it out to me.

"No, I'm good. And before you go any further, will you go somewhere and put on some clothes? Damn! It ain't appropriate for no mother to be standing here talking to her son with his dick hanging. Not to mention that the condom is wet and dripping with cum."

Honey let out a cackling laugh, then sat back on the couch. He rested his arms on top of it, ignoring my request.

"Here's what's up," he said. "You know that li'l comment you made earlier about knocking Karrine off if she started tripping? Well, she started tripping. I had to shut her down for a minute. She should be all good by now, but the last time I checked on her, she was still in some pain."

I knew exactly what comment Honey was talking about. My heart had already dropped to my stomach. I never wanted to see any of my children hurt, and I knew that if Honey had done something to Karrine it was basically because he felt as if he had no other choice.

Honey told me exactly what had happened while I paced the floor. I had even walked over to the bar to pour myself a drink.

"So, let me get this straight. You done shot the shit out of my child, and now you're down here rocking this other bitch's pussy to sleep? I mean, where in the fuck is the remorse, Honey? Obviously, Karrine didn't mean shit to you."

"She does, but you told me to back off that. I did and I got bored. You know a nigga like me got to take care of my needs, so why you acting all brand new? I don't want you to be upset with me, but if Karrine had left this house, she may have caused some damage. She had overheard our conversation, so I had to explain that shit to her."

"It was cool to share some shit with her, but did you have to tell her everything? I'm not too happy about this, Honey. Where is she?"

"She's upstairs. A nurse is up there with her and so is yo' girl, Trice. The bullet went into Karrine's shoulder. She lost a lot of blood. She gon' make it, so no worries."

"I wish I didn't have to, but this shit with Karrine is driving me nuts. I'm going upstairs to check on her. And if you're going to join me, be sure to put on some clothes."

"I will, as soon as I go finish up and knock some of this stress off me. I don't want to keep the woman waiting."

"I don't see what the rush is, because that bitch didn't seem like she was bringing you any excitement. But that's your business, not mine. I'm just saying."

Honey laughed and stood up to stretch. I turned around, not wanting to look at him. "Sometimes, I have to work with what I got," he said. "This is only temporary, or, at least until Karrine gets well."

I quickly turned around, but kept my eyes level with his. "Don't play, nigga. Know what lane to stay in and keep it moving with that other bitch. Like you said, she's waiting."

Honey headed upstairs, whistling as if he had no worries. Unfortunately, I did. I shot vodka to the back of my throat, then went upstairs to go see Karrine.

Since Honey lived in a six-bedroom house, I wasn't sure which room to go into, so I looked inside the first three that I saw. The third bedroom was where Karrine was. There was a night light on, as well as a TV. A nurse sat in one chair, asleep, and Trice sat in another. She was 'sleep, too, and so was Karrine. Two IV's were stuck in her arm, and the right side of her arm and shoulder was wrapped in bandages. A bruised lump was on her forehead, along with a deep cut. Her lips looked dry and her skin appeared pale. Karrine had natural beauty, though, and without a drop of makeup on, she was very pretty.

I woke up the nurse and Trice, asking them to leave the room. The nurse left right away, but Trice stopped to give me a hug.

"She'll be okay," Trice said. "I've been keeping my eyes on her and I'm not going to let her out of my sight. You know if you need anything, just let me know."

"I will," I said, watching Trice walk out of the room.

Trice was my girl, and she was definitely somebody I trusted with my life. I knew with her here, Karrine was in good hands.

I stood next to the bed, looking at Karrine. My thoughts turned to when she was just a little baby and how busy she used to be. Then I thought about how feisty she was growing up and all the difficulties I used to have with her in high school. She wasn't necessarily a bad child, but she did challenge me a lot. Challenged me more than anybody had done, and I guess that was why I had the hardest time dealing with her. She was stubborn in a sense, just like me.

"Karrine," I said, whispering her name.

She was sitting comfortably in bed with a Sleep Number mattress that was adjusted in a way that she could rest. All she did was shift her head to the other side when I called her name, but she didn't open her eyes.

I figured that she probably needed her rest, so I placed a soft kiss on her forehead and sat in one of the leather chairs. I picked up the remote and flipped through several channels, trying to see what was on TV. I settled on a BET movie and started to watch it. Fifteen minutes in, my cell phone rang. When I looked to see who the caller was, it was Chyna. I put the phone up to my ear.

"What do you want?" I asked. "Shouldn't you be somewhere sleep or entertaining your clients?"

She laughed. "I'm in between gigs, and I wanted to call to see what was up with you Miss Lady. You haven't been here all day and I bet you've been somewhere gettin' yo' freak on, haven't you?"

"No, your brother is the one who gets his freak on. I just get my fuck on, but unfortunately, I haven't been able to do so in a long time."

"Yeah, right. I don't believe that for one minute, but oh well. I was just tryin' to find out if or when you were comin' home tonight. I also wanted to know if you've heard from Karrine? I've been callin' her all day, but ain't got no answer yet. I hope she's okay."

"She's fine. I got her taking care of some business for me."

"What kind of business? Is she still with Honey?"

"Yes and no, but I'll tell you all about it when I get home. I probably won't be there until the morning."

"Okay, then. I'ma g'on ahead and get back to work. I made a killin' tonight, and I picked up two more clients. One of them is kind of cute, but the other one is ugly as fuck. It was kind of hard lookin' at him on the screen, but the good thing is I made him laugh, smile, and nut. We both are satisfied, so that's what's up."

"Well, go ahead and make that paper. And you know we don't give a damn how they look, as long as their money is green and they can't touch you."

"Amen to that. See you tomorrow, and before you come home, stop to get me some barbecue potato chips. I've been cravin' some so bad."

"Craving? You ain't pregnant, are you?"

"Uh, no. I'm crampin' right now and I should be on my period in a few more days. Now, about those chips. . . ."

"Please."

"Please, Mama. I love you so very much and you are the best mama ever! Will you bring me those chips, pretty please?"

"No, because I can't stand fake bitches. Good-bye."

Chyna laughed. "And a diet soda, too!"

I hung up on her and shook my head. When I turned to Karrine, her eyes were opened and she was staring at me.

"How are you feeling?" I asked.

"How do you think I'm feelin'?" she asked softly. "And why are you askin'? You don't really care, do you?"

See, I knew this was going to turn ugly because Karrine was always negative and stirring up shit.

I stood up and walked over to the bed. "I do care, but I'm not going to spend the rest of my life trying to convince you that I do. What in the hell is going on with you, Karrine? Why are you trying to be so damn difficult? I thought we squashed this shit, but you keep running over here to Honey making noise."

"The question is not what's goin' on with me, but rather what in the hell is goin' on with you? Honey told me a lot of stuff, and I find it hard to believe that you've been keepin' so much stuff from us, yet you want us to be open and honest with you about everything. This is too much right now, and all I want to do is get the fuck away from here and be done with it."

"So you now know a lot of *stuff* about me that you didn't know before. Girl, I could spend the next week telling you things about me that you don't already know, and that *stuff* will shock the shit out of you. But I don't tell you, because a lot of things are better off left in the past, and it's not in your best interest to know about the business side of things that I conduct with Honey. As for you wanting to get the fuck away from here, that's your choice. But if or when you leave, all I ask is that you keep your fucking mouth shut, and that you do not go around spreading my business. Doing so will get you hurt, and it also may get some people in trouble who I don't want to be in trouble. Got it?"

"I guess you're talkin' about Honey. He's the only person you really care about. I can't believe that you told him to kill me. You gave him permission to do this to me. What kind of mother are you to condone some mess like this? You are a very poor excuse for a mother—and just so you know, yo' parentin' skills suck."

"Yeah, your mouth sucks, too, but I guess that ain't about shit either, because Honey is in his bedroom right now fucking somebody else. I'm a damn good mother, Karrine, who is getting sick and tired of your shit. You always griping about who I care about and who the fuck are my favorites. I don't have any favorites—the truth is, all of you muthafuckas can kiss my ass and go to hell. If you want a goddamn soccer mom who lives in the perimeters of a white picket fence, that ain't me. If you want a good ole church-going mother who reads bedtime stories to her grown-ass kids, wipe their asses for them when they shit, and sit idly by when their kids slap them in their fucking faces, that ain't me either. If I haven't lived up to your expectations as a mother, too damn bad, because you ain't lived up to mine as a daughter. Now, I'm sorry that Honey had to pull the trigger, but you damn lucky that he didn't blow an extra hole up yo' ass. I hope you feel better, and I guess I will see you when you get home. If not, so be it."

I turned to walk away, but Karrine yelled after me. "I'm not coming home, and don't even think about comin' to look for me when I'm gone, because I will be far, far away from here."

I swung around with wrinkles lining my forehead and clapped my hands. "Good, bitch. What do you want me to do? Fall down on my knees and start crying? Hell, no, Karrine, let me repeat . . . that ain't me. I'll tell you what—"

I stormed out of the room and hurried down the hallway and into Honey's bedroom at the end of the hallway. As I busted through the double doors, he had the white chick kneeled on his California King bed while fucking the shit out of her doggie style. She was really getting her clown on now, but I was too upset to comment on her lack of skills.

Honey snapped his head to the side to look at me. "Damn, don't you know how to knock?" he asked.

"Don't you know when to stop fucking? How about right now? I need your help with something. Put on a robe or something—and bring your checkbook with you."

"Now?" he griped.

All these disobedient kids were working me. I tried to be nice, but this was ridiculous. I took off my shoe and flung it at his ass, hitting him in the head.

"The next shoe will be aimed at her. Get out of that nasty coochie and come in here where I need you."

I left the room, hoping that Honey would do like I told him to. I waited outside of the room Karrine was in, and less than five minutes later, Honey came out of his bedroom with a white, fluffy bath towel wrapped around him. I could tell he was mad by the frown on his face, but I seriously did not care.

I went into the room where Karrine was and Honey followed behind me with the checkbook in his hand. Karrine looked past me and glared at him.

"I want you to know that you will pay for this," she said with attitude, but in a soft tone. "I can't believe you did this."

Honey didn't say a word, and unlike me, he wasn't about to argue with Karrine. "Karrine wants to follow the yellow brick road and go far, far away from here. At this point, I don't care if she runs off to Ethiopia and never comes back. Please write her a check that will take care of all of her expenses. I don't want her to come crawling back on her knees, so make sure you write the check for a suitable amount."

Honey pondered and sucked his teeth.

"I don't want your goddamn money," Karrine said, then massaged her shoulder and squinted from the pain. "I'll be able to handle me, trust me on that."

I pointed my finger at her. "Bitch, shut up. I'm trying to buy you out of my life, so I must make this good."

Honey wrote out a check and handed it to me. It was for a hundred thousand dollars, but I ripped it up and let the pieces fall to the floor.

"Nigga, what the fuck is that supposed to do? Can you live off of that amount of money? Hell no."

All he did was shrug. I snatched the checkbook from Honey's hand and wrote the check myself. It was for one million dollars, made out to Karrine Douglas. I ripped the check from the checkbook and laid it on her lap.

"Take it or leave it, I don't care. Your shit at home will be packed and delivered to you tomorrow. Your number will be blocked from ever contacting me again, and your poor piss ass mother never wants to see you again."

I turned to walk out, but Honey grabbed my arm. "Stop this," he said in a calm manner. "You know she needs you, as we all do."

"Well, all I need is a hot-ass bath, a good shit, and a joint. Until we speak again, I'm out of here."

I got the fuck out of there, but like the sorry-ass mother that I was, I stopped at a liquor store to get Chyna her chips and a soda. I even threw in Simone some peanuts and wine coolers, knowing damn well that neither of them would appreciate it.

# KARRINE

## 2

I was glad that Mama was gone, and what she had said to me went in one ear and out the other. She just didn't understand how I was feeling, nor did she seem to care. I wasn't going to complain about the check for a million dollars, and you best believe that after all of the pain and suffering I had been through, this check was worth it.

My body was aching so badly, and whenever I moved it hurt even worse. I tried to sit up, but even that was difficult to do. Honey stood looking at me as if I was the worse child on this earth. I viewed him as a fake-ass nigga, as well as a killer.

"Why are you still standin' there lookin' at me? You can leave now and be sure to tell your mother that I said thanks for the check and I will be cashin' it. It's not gon' bounce, is it?"

"I'm not going to answer yo' stupid question, but before I leave, can I get you anything?"

"Don't try to be nice to me, nigga. You'd better hope that it takes me a minute to get well because I promise you that I'm goin' to deal with you in my own way."

Honey came up to the bed and stood next to me.

"Your threats do not scare me, so you're wasting your time. I'll get you some pain meds, in hopes that they knock you out and allow you some time to think about all this bullshit you've been spilling. I'm real disappointed in you Karrine, and I always thought you were that smarter sister. I guess I was wrong."

I was about to respond to his comment, but a knock on the door silenced me. Honey and me looked at the door, and when it came open, it was a white chick with a silk red robe on.

"I'm so sorry to interrupt," she said. "But I was wondering if I should go or if everything is, uh, cool right now."

"Go," Honey said. "I'll give you a call later."

With a disappointed look on the chick's face, she closed the door. I assumed she was the chick Mama had mentioned who was in another room fucking Honey. This whole thing made me sick to my stomach. I was very jealous, and that was why I needed to get away from all of this. I now had more money to do as I wished, so after another day, maybe two, I was getting the fuck out of here.

"As I was getting ready to say . . . I'm sorry that you're disappointed in me, but after seeing that chick, I'm even more disappointed in you. Why don't you just go ahead and get out of here, Honey? I'm so done with this and I do not feel comfortable being in the presence of a nigga who tried to kill me."

"If I had wanted to kill you, trust me, you would be dead. You did more harm to yourself by falling to the floor and hitting your head. And it ain't my fault if you're clumsy."

"The force from the bullet you fired into me is what knocked me down. This has nothin' to do with me bein' clumsy and yo' ass knows it. Now, please, get the fuck out of here. I have nothin' else to say to you."

Honey walked away and went into the bathroom. Minutes later, he came back with two pills and a glass of water. He gave me the water and both of the pills. I looked at the pills in my hand then tossed the water right in his face.

"Fuck you and these pills! Get out."

Honey removed the towel from around his waist and stood naked as he wiped the water from his face. I could tell he was mad, but he remained calm.

"If you throw away those pills, I'm not going to give you anymore. That pain is going to get real intense when those drugs wear off, and I'm just telling you that for your own good."

He walked off, and I had to turn my head just so I wouldn't admire him from the backside. I hoped his bitch was gone and I couldn't wait to feel better so I could check out of here. I closed my eyes and did my best to go back to sleep.

I woke up to a burst of sun beaming through the room. I could barely crack my eyes it was so bright, but I managed to open them wide when I could feel pain in my shoulder and arm. One side of my body felt stiff, so I did my best to move, just to make sure I wasn't paralyzed. I was in a lot of pain, but when I looked for the pills that were in my hand before I had gone to sleep, I couldn't find them. I also had to pee, so I tried to get out of bed, but it was very difficult to do.

The first thing that I had to do was remove the IVs from my arm. I tightly squeezed my eyes and pulled the small needles out of me. Ever since I was a little girl, I'd hated needles. I told myself that those IVs wouldn't enter me again, and I meant that shit.

The pink nightgown I had on was something an old lady would wear, and I had not a clue how it got on me. Either way, I gripped my arm and turned sideways to get off the bed. My body felt so weak, but I wasn't about to sit there and pee on myself. Therefore, I scooted to the edge of the bed and placed my feet on the soft beige carpet. The room I was in was spacious and decked out in one of my favorite colors, gold. Burgundy was the other color, and everything matched fairly well.

I stood up, but unfortunately not for long. I couldn't keep my balance, and my legs had buckled underneath me. The fall caused more pain to throb in my shoulder and arm. I wanted to call out for help, but I refused to do it.

Instead, using one of my hands to hold me up, and my shaky knees, I crawled on the floor. When I was almost to the bathroom, the bedroom door came open, and Honey stood in the doorway looking at me. He rocked a white sweat suit with a black wife beater underneath it.

"If you needed some help, all you had to do was push the button on that remote control. Here, let me show you."

Honey didn't bother to help me off the floor. Instead, he went over to the bed and picked up the remote. He flipped the TV to a certain channel that showed his office.

"See. Say hello to me. I can see you and you can see me. When you talk, I can hear you. I can see you other ways too, and by those frowns on your face, it looks like you're in pain. Do you want some more pain meds?"

I rolled my eyes and kept it moving to the bathroom. Honey walked behind me, and when I got there and tried to pull myself up on the toilet, I couldn't. My body was too weak and stiff as a board.

Honey bent over and scooped me off the floor then sat me on the toilet. My nightgown still covered me, but I had to pee so badly that I didn't bother to lift it up. Peeing was such a relief, and I let out a deep sigh.

"You look like shit," Honey said. "Why don't you take off the nightgown and let me give you a bath? I'll have the nurse remove those bandages and I'll be happy to get those pills for you."

"Stop tryin' to be nice to me, please. I'm not goin' to ever forgive you for this, and a bath is the least thing you can do for me."

While I remained on the toilet, Honey turned on the waterfall faucets in the Jacuzzi tub. He added bubbles, then left the room. When he came back, the nurse who had been sitting in the chair yesterday was with him.

"Carefully remove her bandages," Honey said to her. "She's going to take a bath. After she's done you can wrap her shoulder again."

This time, I didn't complain. I needed a hot bath, and maybe it would help to soothe some of the soreness in my body. The nurse opened my nightgown and carefully removed the bloody bandages as Honey had told her. She looked at my back and lightly touched where the bullet hole had entered.

"It's going to be a while before this heals, so do not put your entire body in the tub. Just blot yourself with warm water and let me know when you're done."

All I did was nod. She left the bathroom, but Honey stayed.

"Stand up," he said. "Ain't you finished on the toilet yet?"

"Been finished, but I got it from here. I told you I didn't need your help. You can get me those pills, though."

Honey opened the medicine cabinet and got the pain meds for me. I stood up to take off my nightgown, but could barely stand. Honey wrapped his arms around me and held me up.

"Why am I so weak like this?" I questioned.

"Drugs. Removing the bullet wasn't easy and the doctor had to make sure you stayed sleep. You know you're nowhere near one hundred, so just cool out and let me do some things for you."

"Why? Because yo' ass feel guilty?"

"Honestly, no. I don't."

"Well, you should."

Honey unbuttoned the rest of my nightgown and dropped it to the floor. I hoped he got a whiff of my piss and I'm sure he did. He bent over and swiped the nightgown from the floor. Before standing straight up, he pecked my midsection with his lips.

"Sexy," he said. "Too bad you fucked around and got shot. If not, I would be getting me some of that pussy right now."

"Tuh. I'm glad you think so, but I'm here to tell you that it ain't goin' down like that with us no more. Never, ever again, and I can promise you that."

I slowly walked over to the tub, wondering how I was going to get in. I didn't want to slip, fall, and break something.

"I'm not convinced yet," Honey said, carefully lifting me. He slowly lowered me into the tub filled with bubbles. I had to admit that it felt really good.

"Remember what the nurse told you. Don't lean all the way back into the water, and blot yourself with the towel. I'm going to take Trice some clothes to wash and then I'll be back."

I didn't say anything, but when Honey left the bathroom, I wondered how I could still have feelings for him, especially after what he'd done. He was the one who had told Mama about what I'd said about her. He kept shit going between Mama and me by doing that, and then to shoot me was the worst thing possible.

But there I was, thinking about him. I was thinking about Mama too, and she'd made me so upset when she was here that I wanted to scream. I wanted to cry, too, but I couldn't even do that. I missed my sisters and I knew they were worried about me. But as soon as I got my strength back, I was going to make some moves that would shock them all.

After downing the pills that Honey had given to me, I squeezed the soapy rag on my body and washed myself. With my eyes closed, I thought about everything from the million dollars to where I would ultimately move. Yeah, Cali had always been the dream for my final destination, but now I was thinking of somewhere quiet like Colorado or Nebraska. I even thought about moving out of the country, just to get away from everyone. It was definitely an option, and in a few more days I would make my decision.

As I was in deep thought, Honey came back into the bathroom. He stood next to the tub, looking down on me.

"How you doing in here?" he asked.

"I'm fine, but I would like some privacy, if you don't mind."

"Privacy? Why? So you can play with yourself?" He kneeled down next to the tub and pulled one of the clean towels from the rail. "You don't have to do that, especially when I can do that for you."

"Don't touch me, Honey. I mean it."

He dipped the towel in the warm water and lathered it with soap. "And if I do touch you, what are you going to do about it? It's not like you can do much about it, so shut the fuck up and thank me later."

Honey washed my back with the towel, very careful not to touch my wound. I let him do it, only because the shit felt good. I closed my eyes as he went from my back, to my breasts. From my breasts, to my legs. From my legs to my thighs, and from my thighs to my pussy. That was when I grabbed the rag and opened my eyes.

"I got that. Thank you very much."

"Are you sure? You know I don't mind taking care of that for you too."

I gazed into his eyes, wanting so badly to pull on his locs and drag his ass into the tub with me. I couldn't believe my thoughts of fucking him. Shame on me. I was sure he could read me, but I wasn't about to give in.

"I'm positive. Now, please leave me in peace."

Honey stood up and I saw his dick imprint that had swelled in his sweatpants. I was going to comment, but decided against it. He tried to be funny by pulling his dick out so I could see it. I winced and rolled my eyes.

"If you don't mind, I have to drain the vein. Turn your head and don't look at it, a'ight?"

What I did was not pay him no mind. I wanted to fall asleep in the tub, but I knew I couldn't. For the next thirty minutes or so, I chilled and stayed in thought. I had to do something that would make Mama hate me more, that would leave me walking away from this with some kind of satisfaction. Yeah, the money was good, but I didn't want Mama to think that she could buy me out of her life, per her own words.

The problem, however, was Simone and Chyna. I didn't want them to hate me. I didn't want them to feel as though I had betrayed them. But this wasn't about them. It was about me. My sanity. My peace. And my happiness.

I was ready to get out of the tub, but Honey was nowhere to be found. The pain medicine had kicked in, but I was still feeling a little weak. Unfortunately, I had to stay in the tub until someone came to get me. That was almost ten minutes later, and it was Honey. He had a towel thrown over his shoulder and lotion was in his other hand.

He bent down next to me. "Put your arm around my neck and hold on tight."

I put my arm around his neck and he lifted me from the tub. Water dripped from my body as he carried me out of the bathroom and into the bedroom. He laid me on the bed and dried my body with the towel. Afterward, he squeezed lotion in his hand, but I shook my head.

"You've already done enough. Thanks."

"But I'm not finished yet. Let me soften you up."

"I'm already soft, with or without a hole in my shoulder. Please find me another nightgown or somethin' to put on. In the meantime, I'll take care of the lotion."

Honey ignored me and wiped the lotion on my leg. I reached out to slap him, but he grabbed my wrist.

"Grow up, Karrine. Cut the bullshit and do not put your fucking hands on me. Please don't make me repeat myself again."

I snatched my hand away from him. I swear I wanted to hurt this nigga for what he'd done, but ol' stupid me had a soft spot for him. He rubbed the lotion between his hands, and then walked over to a closet where there were a few pieces of pajama pants and two nightgowns hanging. He pulled out a white one with flowers on it that buttoned down the middle. I sat up in bed as he took his time putting the nightgown on me. He fluffed my pillows and straightened and adjustened my bed. I sat, watching him go to the closet to get some house shoes. He removed the price tag from them and placed them on my feet. Afterward, he laid the remote on my lap.

"The nurse will be back in to patch you up. Trice will bring you something to eat in a little while, and if you need me, change the channel to three and speak."

Honey was getting ready to walk out of the room, but I wanted to fuck with him. "Can you do me a favor and rub my feet with lotion? I don't think I can reach them, but the rest of my body should be okay."

He hesitated, but came over to the bed. He removed my house shoes and oozed lotion into his hand again. He began to massage my feet, and even though it felt good, I pretended that it felt magnificent.

"Oooo, mmmm, ahhhh, right there is just how I like it," I moaned. "Keep it right there and press a little bit harder. Harder, Honey, harder!"

I had a smirk on my face while Honey's look remained stern. When he got done rubbing my feet, he got on the bed and crawled his way up to me like a tiger. His lips were only a few inches from mine and so were his eyes.

"How many days do you think that it's going to be before you get well? I don't want to fuck with you right now because the many positions I want to put you in may hurt you."

"I'm not sure about that, but I am sure about this. There's a gash in my shoulder, compliments of you. I don't feel comfortable lying on my back and allowing you to get creative with another hole, if you know what I mean. And didn't your mother tell you to leave me the fuck alone? I know you wouldn't ignore her wishes. I'm sure she'll make you pay for it if you do."

"Like I've taken care of the hole in your shoulder this morning, I can take good care of the other one too. As for your mother, she truly knows where my heart is, so I doubt that she'll trip. And even if she does, I'm a grown man and I can handle myself. So just think about what I said, and hit me up whenever you feel ready. I'm game when you are. Bet?"

I opened my mouth, but Honey covered it with his. He sucked my lips, but when his tongue went further into my mouth, I backed away. He licked his lips and hit me with a crooked smile. "Sweet," he said. "So, very, sweet."

Honey got off the bed and left the room, leaving me speechless. I couldn't help but to think about his proposal, but a few other things shook up my mind. For one, I was hungry as fuck. Trice had finally come into the room with a tray that had fruit, a Belgian waffle, orange juice, and some bacon. I could probably get used to this, but then again, I know I needed to hurry up and get the fuck out of there.

"Would you like for me to cut up your waffle for you?" Trice asked.

"If you don't mind."

"Not at all."

She cut up my waffle and poured syrup on top of it.

"You know, you shouldn't have removed those IVs from your arm. They help you get well, you know? I'm going to have the nurse come back in to put them back in."

"No, you won't. I don't want them back in, so please don't send her in here again to stick me. I would appreciate that very much."

Trice didn't say anything, and all she did was slowly nod her head. I couldn't wait to tear into the food, but I waited until she'd left the room. As soon as she closed the door, I got busy and gobbled up the food like I hadn't eaten in days. I then thought about Honey watching me, so I picked up the remote and turned it to channel three.

"Damn, slow down," he said. "You gon' choke yourself."

I looked around the room, even up at the ceiling to see if I could find the camera.

"Don't waste your time," Honey said. "You'll never find it."

"Okay, but why are you watchin' me. Can't I have some kind of privacy while I'm here?"

"No, you can't. I was told to keep my eyes on you, so that's what I'm doing."

"So, in other words, I'm your prisoner. Is that what you're sayin'?"

"Nope. Not at all. You are free to walk out of that front door, anytime you're ready to. I suspect that will be soon, because you're starting to look better already."

"The pain medicine really helped, and I'm gon' need a few more of those before you get too busy. I'm also gon' need some more syrup, so when you get around to it, why don't you bring me some?"

"I'll have Trice bring it to you, but since you're making all of these requests, I have a few requests too."

I sipped from the orange juice and bit a piece of bacon before responding. "I kind of know what your requests revolve around, but I told you that ain't happenin'. If it's somethin' other than that, tell me."

"It is something other than that, so this should be easy. I want to see how you get down for the niggas who be watching you on the screen. Pretend that I've paid for your services and show me how you do it."

"Nigga, are you crazy? You don't have enough money to pay this money-makin' mama right here, and I work for no one for free."

"Free? I've been catering to you all morning, and I've had my girls take good care of you. Ain't that payment enough?"

"No, it's not. But if you want me to show you somethin', I'll be happy to show you the bullet hole—"

"Yeah, yeah, yeah . . . whatever. I already saw it, and you act like I shot you with my Glock 9. I only hit you up with a .22 Smith & Wesson, and like I said, had you not been so clumsy, you wouldn't even be in this predicament." He moved closer to the screen and laughed. "How's your head doing? It looks like the swelling has gone down a little."

My mouth dropped open from his insults. I didn't see this shit as funny, so I clicked off the TV and continued to eat my food. A few minutes later, Trice came in with the syrup. And after that, the nurse came back into the room, trying to explain why she wanted me to have the IVs back in my arm. I wasn't completely sold on it, but anything to help me get better.

For the next two days, I worked my way back to better health. The pain pills are what helped me, and so did all of the catering that the nurse, Trice, and Honey had done. I was nowhere near one hundred yet, but was feeling better. Maybe because Mama had done what she said she was going to do, and that was have all of my clothes delivered to Honey's place. She didn't lie about that, and Trice and Honey took their time bringing all of my things to the room.

"So, where do you go from here?" Honey said, standing near the doorway with his hands in his pockets. "I know you're not going to stay, and since you're feeling better, I guess it's just a matter of time, right?"

"You're right. I've been thinkin' a lot these past few days, and I really and truly think it's best that I move on. Kind of start over and do my own thing. You have my word that I won't say anything else about what you told me, and I'm gon' do my best to forget about our little incident, too."

"So that means that you forgive me for shooting you, right?"

"What it means is that you should regret doin' what you did to me. I asked you before and you said no. Do you still feel that way?"

Honey didn't hesitate. "Absolutely not. I don't regret it, Karrine, because had you walked out of here, and we hadn't had this opportunity to talk, there ain't no telling what you would have done. I had to protect myself, as well as . . . Mama."

I rolled my eyes and sighed from his response. This was why I couldn't even forgive Honey if I wanted to. Him having no regrets meant that he would happily do it again, and that didn't sit right with me. I was trying not to feel bitter about this, but his words, and the fact that Mama didn't seem to be the least bit concerned, pissed me off.

"I'm leavin' tomorrow," was all I said, then sat back on the bed.

"Thanks for letting me know. Tell me what time so I can call you a taxi to pick you up."

"Taxi? My car is still outside, ain't it?"

"Per the request of your mother, she said that that car was hers. Said it was purchased with her money, not yours, and that you now have enough money to buy your own car. You may want to search the Internet for a new car. Shall I bring you a laptop?"

Honey seemed like he thought the shit was funny, but I didn't. If that was how it was going down, cool. I'd buy me a fucking new car and these motherfuckers around here could kiss my ass.

"To hell with a laptop. Just bring me a phone so I can call my sisters. Better yet, where is my cell phone at?"

"Sorry. That's been held up too. Since your mother pays the cell phone bills, she wanted me to make sure I kept your phone. You have plenty of money to get you a new one."

I glared at Honey with an evil stare. "Get the hell out of here, please. And if you talk to your mother, be sure to tell her I said she can kiss my big ole juicy ass."

"No problem. I'll tell her."

Honey got ready to close the door and I yelled out after him. "I'm sure you will, bastard! You tell her everything else!"

He kept it moving and didn't say nothing else. Minutes later, Trice brought me a cordless phone, and I called Chyna first. I got no answer, so I called Simone. Thankfully, she answered. It felt good to hear her voice, so I had a big Kool-Aid smile on my face.

"What's been up, chica?" I asked with excitement.

"Nothing much, girl." Her voice sounded flat.

"If it ain't nothin', why you soundin' like that?"

"Because, Karrine, there is so much goin' on right now. Mama around here all upset about you and her not gettin' along, and then she talkin' about your leavin' us. All of your stuff is gone and you haven't called us to say one word. Then, what's up between you and Honey? Chyna told me some stuff that I'm findin' very hard to believe."

"First off, I don't want to discuss Mama because she is wrong on so many different levels. I know how you and Chyna feel about her, but I feel a different way. Please respect that, all right? Secondly, I was wrong for not callin' y'all, but I've been down for several days because your mother told your brother to kill me. He shot me while I was tryin' to get the fuck out of here, and to make a very long story short, it is a must that I get away. I can't do this anymore, Simone. I love y'all and everything, but this situation with Mama and Honey is too much for me. She's not tellin' y'all everything, and I don't feel as if I should have to be the one to share what is really goin' on with her. That's your mother, and it's her job to tell y'all what's up. As far as me and Honey goes, yes, I was fuckin' him, but damn sure not anymore. That's a long story too, but I don't want to talk about all of that right now. I just want to say that I'm leavin' tomorrow and I don't have a clear destination yet. I promise to call, though, and let you and Chyna know what's up with me. But y'all have to promise not to tell Mama where I'll be. Please understand that I just don't want her in my business."

Simone was quiet for a few minutes, but then she spoke up. "You know I'm goin' to miss you, and please don't ask me to understand anything, because I don't. Especially when I don't have all of the facts, but if you want to move on to bigger and better things, who am I to stop you? I love you no matter what, and don't you ever forget that, all right?"

"I love you, too. Always. Now, where is Chyna at? I called her, but she didn't answer her phone."

"She's in the shower. I'll tell her to call you back when she gets out."

"No, tell her I'll call her. I no longer have my cell phone, so I'll have to call her back. Other than that, what else has been up with you? How's business?"

"Business is good, but I do have myself a little problem. I'm just not sure how to handle it right now and I'm startin' to get a little worried."

"What's up? Tell me."

"Well, I kind of did somethin' that I wasn't supposed to do a while back, and I met with this nigga I was hookin' up with through the video thing online. You know what we did to Honey, I kind of did that to him and he's been sendin' me threatenin' messages and shit. I think it's him stalkin' me, but I'm worried, because he now knows my real name, he knows where we live, and he knows about y'all too. I was goin' to say somethin' to Mama, but she's been so on edge lately that I'm afraid she will blow the fuck up. She may also shut this video porn shit down and stop me and Chyna from makin' paper. I would hate for her to do that, and I can't figure out if this nigga just fuckin' with me or if his ass is for real."

My heart had started to beat faster. "Simone, how long has that shit been goin' on?"

"For about a week and a half now. He's been sendin' me more and more messages, sayin' that today is the day I will die. That's why I haven't been nowhere. I'm kind of scared to leave the house, but I don't like the fact that this nigga got me livin' in fear."

"Simone, please do me a favor and tell Chyna about this. If you don't want to tell Mama, fine. But you should have said somethin' when that shit started, especially if he has our real information. Do you know his full name?"

"I still got his driver's license and I do know where he lives. But the problem is that I can't really say that it's him. I don't want to do nothin' until I know for sure who's fuckin' with me."

"I feel you, but give me that nigga's name, his address, and any other information you have on him. Whatever you do, don't leave the house, and please tell Chyna what's been goin' on. I'ma see what I can do on my end, and I'll let you know what I find out in a day or two. Hang tight and do not let no motherfucker scare you like that, all right?"

"I'm tryin' not to, but it is what it is."

Simone and I talked for a few more minutes, and even though I didn't let her know how I felt deep inside, I was worried too. When we got off the phone, I spent the next few hours, trying to find out how I could help Simone with this situation. I wanted to get the fuck out of here and run, but I couldn't run under these conditions.

Around 9:00 p.m., I was done packing most of my things to go. My shoulder was feeling a little achy, and I had a slight headache from my conversation with Simone.

I stripped naked and then moved one of the chairs right in front of the screen. I turned the channel to number three and could see Honey sitting at his desk with his head lowered. The rap music in the background was pretty loud, and he was bobbing his head while writing something down on paper.

At first, I whispered his name and he didn't look up. My voice got louder and that was when his head snapped up and his eyes widened when he saw me sitting naked through the screen. I sat up straight and crossed one of my legs over the other.

"What'cha doin'?" I asked.

"Truthfully," he said.

"Yep. Truthfully."

"Trying to figure out who the fuck owe me money and how much. I got three niggas who done came up short, and I want to make sure it's not my error before I start making some calls and showing my ass."

"Thanks for bein' honest, but that sounds so borin'. I thought you may have a little time to play, but if you don't, I understand."

Honey laid his pen on the desk and placed his index finger along the side of his face. "I always have time to play," he said. "Besides, I could use a break."

"Good. Me too."

I uncrossed my legs and spread them wide on the arms of the chair. I then slid three fingers into my mouth and sucked them as if they were a fat dick. When I pulled my fingers out, I moved my index finger in a come here motion, meaning for Honey to come to my pussy, right along with my fingers. I used one finger to twirl around my clit, trying to stir my juices so he could see them. He didn't see anything until I slipped several fingers into my hairless slit and grinded my pussy while rotating my fingers inside of me. A light glaze had started to build, and I could feel the liquids slowly dripping through the crack of my ass.

"Can you see it?" I asked Honey. "It's this wet because I can't stop thinkin' about fuckin' you. How long are you goin' to make me pretend that these fingers inside of me are your dick? I love pretendin', but damn, Honey. Help a sista out, would you?"

Honey attentively stared at me through the screen. He then removed his finger from the side of his face and folded his arms in front of him. I sucked in my bottom lip and picked up the speed of my rotating fingers that I started to jab quickly into my pussy, moaning while doing it. The speedy thrusts made me grind harder. The harder I grinded the more excited I became. My pussy was about to spit hella cum, and if anybody knew how to hit my hot spots, it was me. I kept my eyes on it, watching my cherry grow harder as I turned it with my thumb and seeing more glaze appear on my fingers.

"I . . . I wish you were here to suck this shit that's about to rain from my pussy. I prefer that it rains on your head, but you can't get to me fast enough, so I'ma have to let my pussy juices go to waste."

I looked at the screen and Honey was gone. A few minutes later, he came busting through the door and dropped right down in front of me. His arms locked around my legs to secure them and he dove in, eating the shit out of me like I was his first meal of the week.

His fierce tongue was so deep inside that I could no longer hang on. I lifted my ass from the chair and Honey rushed to throw my legs over his shoulders. I screamed out, wanting to cry so badly because his pussy sucking skills were on point.

"Fuuuuuuck! Baaaby, daaaaamn!" I cried out, unable to catch my breath. "Do . . . do this puuuusy gooooood and don't stooooop!"

Honey did my pussy major justice. I hated it, too, but he just didn't know how much I needed that right now. I sprayed his lips with more juice than he probably anticipated, but he damn sure wasn't complaining. After I came, he jumped to his feet and snatched off his jeans and boxers. He pulled me up from the chair and didn't seem to care that my shoulder was still a bit tender. I wanted to complain about his aggressiveness but didn't dare. He pushed me back on the bed, causing it to squeak as he laid on top of me and hooked my legs around his back. When I looked into his eyes, he blinked and lowered his head to my breasts to suck them. His dick was poking right at my slit, ready to break it wide open. I squirmed from the way the tip of his tongue toyed with my nipple, and I lifted his head to stop him. I wanted to know what was on his mind, but before I could say anything he licked his lips and spoke up.

"I'm sorry," he said with pain that I had never seen before in his eyes. "Forgive me for what I did to you."

Honey lowered his head again to my breasts, but I raised his head. My eyes searched into his. "I . . . I can't forgive you, but I love yo' ass so goddamn much that this shit is scary. For my own sanity, I just have to get away from you."

A tear slipped from the corner of my eye and Honey kissed it. I could feel his dick split me open and that was when he responded. "Leaving is your choice, not mine. If you have to get away, do so. Just not tonight. Tonight, you belong to me."

You damn right I did. I had been fighting my feelings for Honey for so damn long that it was destroying me. I kept telling myself that this was all about Mama, but it wasn't. It was about the both of them. I hated their connection. I hated that he was my stepbrother even if we didn't share the same blood. I had no goddamn business loving him or fucking him like this. I wanted to stop loving him, but I couldn't. I wanted to end this, but it was so damn hard to walk away. I was upset with Mama because she said no to Honey, but I said yes. Yes, I wanted me some Honey. All of him, but he made me so crazy. He was like a drug to me that I was fighting to let go of. I didn't want to appear weak, foolish or as a stupid bitch who ignored the kind of nigga she was dealing with. I never wanted him to know how much I loved him, but there I was tonight, playing the love game and spilling those words that I was never to say to anyone else, over and over again. As he fucked the shit out of me, I said it louder and louder. Loud enough for him to take it and run with it, and for every goddamn person in the house to hear it. I loved me some Honey, and there wasn't a damn thing that anybody could do, not even a motherfucking bullet, that could change that. Period.

Honey tore into my pussy for what seemed like hours. By the time things started to settle down, it was almost midnight. I lay naked in his arms, feeling awkward but protected. The room was silent and all that was going on between us was a bunch of foot rubbing underneath the sheets. Honey finally pulled away from me and sat up.

"I need to go back downstairs and finish up a few things. I'll be turning in shortly, though, but you know we'll talk more tomorrow before you leave."

I nodded, but couldn't even gather my thoughts to say anything. Honey got out of bed and put his jeans back on. He winked at me before walking out the door and resuming to his business.

I lay in bed, looking up at the ceiling and thinking. My mind was racing a mile a minute, only because I knew there were several issues that I had to resolve. The one thing that I was taught was to do to others, what they did to you. That kept playing in my head, as well as what had happened throughout the night.

After telling Honey that I loved him over and over again, not once . . . not one time did he say it back to me. That shit hurt like hell, and even though the dick was good, it wasn't enough. I wanted him to handle that situation with Simone for me, but I decided to go at it alone. It was the least I could do, and then I would get the fuck out of here for real.

As the clock ticked away, I waited until it was around three o'clock in the morning before I made my next move. I turned on the screen, seeing that Honey's office was now empty. I grabbed a duffle bag with some of my clothes in it and put it on my shoulder. In a dark blue hoodie and jeans, I tiptoed down the hallway and cracked the door to Honey's bedroom. I could see the white sheet resting on his muscular frame and he was sound asleep. I reached for the silencer that was tucked behind me and aimed it right at him on the bed.

While I was deeply in love with Honey, I couldn't let go of the fact that he had not regretted shooting me. At any given chance, he would do it again, per Mama. Next time, I might not be this lucky. I couldn't ignore that he had been causing me so much pain and that he just didn't seem to fucking care about anything but my pussy. It saddened me to do this, and as the tears began to roll down my face, I pulled the trigger. Two bullets pierced his midsection, and I rushed away from the door, closing it behind me.

I moved down the stairs so quickly that when I saw a shadow, it completely caught me off guard. I bumped right into the person, and when I looked up and saw Honey, I staggered backward. He was eating a sandwich.

"So, I guess you were going to leave me without saying good-bye," he said.

I know my skin had to be pale as ever. My eyes were wide and I tried my best to read him. If he wasn't the motherfucker in his bed, who was it? I didn't bother to ask, nor did I reply to him. I rushed out the front door, leaving it wide open and broke out in a sprint. I ran until I couldn't run anymore. Didn't know where I was going, but I just kept on running. Before I knew it, I was miles away from Honey's crib and I felt like I was on the verge of an anxiety attack as I hid underneath some stairs in an apartment complex.

By now, I pictured the scene at Honey's crib. The police were there, and a dead body was being hauled away. Honey was mad as hell, and he probably figured out that the bullet was supposed to be for him. I figured that Mama had been called and the both of them would be out to get me. All of that shit swam in my head, along with the check for a million dollars. It was the only way I could get out of Chicago for good and I knew it. I couldn't wait until the bank opened, just so I could hurry the fuck in there and try to do something with this check, before Mama or Honey shut things down. Unfortunately for me, though, the shit didn't go according to my plans. Somebody had gotten to the bank before I did. A stop payment had been issued on the check, and my own personal account that I used for my video porn services had a negative five-dollar balance. Needless to say, I was ass out. All I could do was sit on the bench at a nearby park and cry my eyes out.

"I'll be muthafuckin' damned!" I shouted and pounded my legs at the same time.

I was supposed to be a survivor, but after living on the streets for almost two weeks, with no place to go, I was starting to lose my mind. I really and truly didn't see how homeless people could do this shit. I found myself, just like them, eating whatever I could find to fill my stomach, stealing food from stores, and laying my head wherever I could.

I had surely fucked up, and I don't think I had cried this much in my entire life. All I'd had to my name was the clothes I'd had in the duffle bag, plus the ones I was wearing. Without a bath or shower, I was starting to smell myself. My shoulder was getting sore, my short hair was starting to get nappy, and my feet were killing me from all of the walking I'd done. I just couldn't walk anymore. I did, however, walk to a nearby shelter that fed the homeless on Sunday morning.

The line was so long, but I had no other choice but to wait. I looked at the people in line, feeling so out of place. No one said anything to each other out of shame and stress . . . basically, each person that I saw exemplified somebody who had had a rough life.

A life that I really didn't know much about. Looking at this shit, I'd had it made. Maybe I did, but I had to do something to get back on my feet. My mind wasn't calculating fast enough what my next move should be, but that was because my stomach needed to be taken care of first.

When I got inside, the food line moved pretty quickly. The people serving the food seemed nice, and they kept smiling at me. I lowered my head in shame, unable to look anyone in the room eye-to-eye. I thanked the last lady who put a carton of apple juice on my tray, and I walked away to find a seat.

I was shocked by how crowded the room was, and so many mothers were there with their children. I began to wonder how those mothers felt having no place to go with their children, or how those children felt sitting in this room with a bunch of weird looking people who probably scared them.

With not too many places to sit, I chose to sit at a table with a woman and two of her kids. She was a black woman who looked pretty decent, but again, you could tell that life had gotten to her. Her nails were dirty, her hair was matted, and the way she was chomping on the food implied that she hadn't eaten in a while. Her kids were getting down too, and when I sat at the table they both looked over at me.

"Do you mind if I sit here?" I asked the lady.

"No, I don't mind at all. Have a seat."

I sat down and couldn't wait to dive into the food that looked pretty good to me. The servers seemed very generous, and they piled my plate with sausage, grits, eggs, and three pancakes. I even had some fruit, too, so I started with that first. The kids kept on eyeing me as I ate, and their stares made me a bit nervous. The little girl's eyes were big and round, and her sandy-brown thick hair was braided in two nappy ponytails. I wanted to take her hair down and comb it myself, but I knew the mother would be offended.

As for the little boy, he was so adorable. His afro was full of naps and there was a bruise underneath his eye. I wondered how it got there, and as I was in deep thought about what this family had been through, I found myself staring at them more than they stared at me. I finally smiled at the little boy and he blushed.

"Boy, eat yo' food and stop flirtin' with that young lady," his mother said.

He swung his legs underneath the table and kept smiling at me. "But she's so pretty Mama. Ain't she pretty?"

His comment made me feel like a million bucks. I had been feeling like shit, and this was the first time I had a smile on my face in quite some time.

"Yes, she is pretty, but please eat yo' food. There ain't no tellin' when we gon' be able to eat again."

Her words put a frown on my face, but I thanked the little boy for his compliment. Knowing that they might not have anything to eat after this broke my heart. Damn, this was so fucked up. I had to find out this woman's story, so I spoke up.

"You have some beautiful kids," I said. "But if you don't mind me askin', why are y'all here? My name is Karrine, by the way. Karrine Douglas."

I extended my hand to the woman and she shook it. "Patricia Simmons," she said. "And I guess we're here for the same reasons you're here. I'm down on my luck and I didn't have any access to food."

"How long has it been like this for you? I mean, you kind of look like you've been really goin' through somethin'."

She sighed and chewed on her food. "I have, but God is good and I know he's goin' to pull me through this. This is only temporary, but I have faith that we'll someday find a home and have all of the food we can eat at our table."

She looked at her kids with a smile, trying to give them hope too. They smiled back at her. I'm sure believing that all would be well.

"I'm a little down on my luck too," I said. "But I should be okay. I know you came here to eat, but where are you stayin'? I don't mean to be nosey or anything, but I just want to know, because I'm lookin' for a place to stay too."

"I'm currently livin' in this shelter, but unfortunately they are full. You may want to try the one about five or six blocks from here. They may be full too, but it's worth a try."

I nodded, and as me and the woman continued to chat with each other, she loosened up and told me how she'd gotten to this point. Bottom line, her husband was on drugs and he took everything they'd had. He abused her, as well as her children. That was why the little boy had a black eye. She had finally left her husband for good, because their situation had never been this bad. She even admitted that her husband had abused her kids before, and said that she'd felt guilty for not leaving him a long time ago.

"I should have left when my baby told me what he'd done to her," she cried and dabbed her eyes with the shirt she was wearing. "I was such a fool. A fool for love, but now I'm payin' the price. But like I said, it's gon' be all right, though. I'll get through this, and I'm never goin' back to that fool again."

I reached across the table and touched the woman's trembling hand. "No need to cry. It will be okay, just hang in there. You and your kids, all right?"

She nodded, and I couldn't believe all of what the woman had told me she had been through. I looked at my situation and wanted to slap myself for thinking that life had dealt me a shitty hand. While I definitely had setbacks, it was nothing like this. It was nothing like what the people around me had probably been through, and I figured that this was my reality check. A big, fucking wakeup call that I needed at this moment in time.

I finished my food, and after telling the nice family that it was a pleasure meeting them, I got up from the table and dumped my tray. I noticed several people staring at me, but I walked up to one of the nice ladies who had served my food earlier.

"Excuse me. Can I talk to you for a minute?" I asked.

"Sure," she said, walking away from the others to see what I wanted. "What can I help you with, young lady?"

"This is kind of embarrassin', but I was wonderin' if there was anywhere around here where I can take a shower? I'm kind of—"

The lady cut me off and told me to follow her. With my duffle bag on my shoulder, I followed behind her to a nearby bathroom. She opened the door and pointed to several showers that lined the wall.

"There's really not much privacy in here, but it is a woman's restroom. I don't know where any towels would be, but maybe you have something in your bag you can use. I hope this helps."

"It does. Thank you."

The woman smiled and left the bathroom. I didn't care who came into the bathroom, I stripped the soiled clothes from my body and hurried into the shower. I couldn't believe how spectacular the warm water felt beating down on my body. I felt like I had died and gone to Heaven, it felt so good. I thought about how crazy it is for some people to not have access to a shower. But it was true, and I was witnessing just how tough out here it really was.

I washed my body with my hands, and after thirty long minutes, the water had turned ice cold on me. I used one of my clean shirts in my duffle bag to dry off with, and chose to put on another pair of jeans and a white wife beater. I went without panties, but I did have another bra.

Almost ten minutes after my shower, I left out the back door and got on my way. I stopped by the other shelter that was only a few blocks away, but they were full too. At this point, I had no idea what I was going to do or where I was going to go. I kept thinking about Mama, my sisters, Honey, the man I had killed in his bedroom, and the lady with those kids. I was starting to realize what a fool I'd been, and this lady's situation didn't seem much different from Mama's. I guess she could have been in a shelter with us too, but she'd somehow made a way out of no way.

With the way Ray had done Mama, we could have been living in a homeless shelter, but we weren't. Those kids would die to live in the house I'd lived in, but then again, so would I right now. But I refused to go back and deal with Mama. I just couldn't do it—and by now, she probably wanted me dead.

For the rest of the day I sat in the park reading a book. I went to the grocery store and stole some food to grub on, and then I sat in front of a bank that I was seriously considering robbing. It was either that, or rob somebody else, just to get some kind of money in my pockets. That was the only way for me to make a move, and with the gun I'd had in my duffle bag, I figured I could get a car, money, or something that would help me get out of the situation of being on the streets.

But for whatever reason, I didn't really want to go that route. Been there, done that. I had ridiculed Mama for taking me down a shaky path, but there I was, contemplating doing bad things. But what other choice did I have? Not many, so when the night crept upon me, I stalked the streets, trying to find my first victim. I lucked up on a black man, driving an expensive car and wearing fine clothes. I suspected that his wallet was fat, and his money and car could be my ticket to the next city.

As I watched my prey from a distance, he was sitting in his car while on the cell phone. His attention seemed focused on the caller, and by the time I rushed up to the car and tapped the window with the gun, he was shocked. The cell phone dropped in his lap and he held his hands in front of him.

My black hoodie covered my head, and I gritted my teeth while holding the gun steady, ready to shoot. "Nigga, put yo' wallet on the seat next to you and slowly get the fuck out of the car. If you try anything stupid, I will blow your fuckin' brains out, so be real careful."

The man lifted himself from the seat and pulled out his wallet, showing it to me before he tossed it on the seat. He then opened the door with ease and put one of his feet on the ground.

"Please don't hurt me," he said in a very calm tone. "You can have whatever you want. Just let me know."

I had to move quickly, because I could see headlights from a car coming. "Four digit password to your credit card with the most money available. I have your information, so don't get tricky, nigga, and give me the wrong shit."

"Seven, one, five, five," he said then slowly moved away from the car.

I kept the gun on him, but as the car with the headlights came closer, the motherfucking sirens came on. I couldn't believe this shit. I had to break out running, fast. I turned to look behind me, and I'll be damned if a police officer wasn't coming from behind me. Mama always said that running track in high school would come in handy one day, and it damn sure did. I cut several corners, trying to hold on to my duffle bag that kept slipping from my shoulder. I bumped into several people and even fell on my ass when I slipped on something wet on the ground. I looked back, and the police were at a distance now. When I turned into an alley, I knew I had lost him. I could hear many police sirens and I knew they were close by. Completely out of breath, I bent over and put my hands on my knees. I took deeps breaths and wiggled my toes that felt as if they were burning inside of my tennis shoes. I didn't know if the coast was clear or not, so I waited. I waited for about an hour and sat low on some concrete steps that led to somebody's basement. Trash was boiling over in a Dumpster, and the smell of the alley made me sick to my stomach.

While on the steps, I searched my duffle bag for my cap and I removed my hoody. I was just about ready to close my bag, when I saw a big-ass rat down by my feet. I jumped up and got the fuck away from those steps. I was nowhere in the clear, and when I hurried down the alley, I saw a white, scraggly-looking man coming my way. Something about him didn't appear to be right, and the wicked look in his shifty eyes said that I'd better quickly move in another direction. The last thing I wanted to do was show fear, but I couldn't help it. This street shit wasn't for me, and it was straight up a goddamn jungle out here.

I lowered my head, trying my best not to make eye contact with the man. But when I attempted to walk by him, he moved over to block my path.

"I need a cigarette," he said, showing his yellow stained rotten teeth. "You got one?"

"No." I tried to go around him, but that didn't work. He grabbed my arm and I couldn't believe how strong the man's grip was. Before I knew it, he shoved me to the ground, and what I'd thought he wanted, he didn't take. What he took was my duffle bag, then he broke out running with it.

It didn't matter to me that he'd had my bag, until I realized that my gun was inside of there. There I was trying to rob somebody, but then I turned around and got robbed my fucking self.

This was truly it for me. It was either call Mama or call Honey. I didn't know who to call first, but I knew that I needed somebody's help. Chyna or Simone would definitely come help me, but I didn't want to risk Simone leaving the house with her stalker on the loose. The more I'd thought about it, with Chyna, she would probably bring Mama with her, and I wasn't so sure that I wanted to deal with Mama right now. That was why I made the decision to reach out to Honey. After making it through one more night, I was going to break down and call him, in hopes that he would be able to help me. I knew it was a big risk to take, but I had to do something.

That night, I didn't even sleep. I had no money, no gun for protection, and no more changing clothes. My eyes were tired in the morning and I felt sick to my stomach. Maybe the fucking food at the homeless shelter was making me sick, or the fact that I hadn't eaten much since yesterday besides a glazed donut that I had found in a bag that was in the trash. I was so woozy that I staggered to a nearby drugstore and asked the young woman behind the register, who looked to be about the same age as me, if she had a phone I could use.

"I'm sorry to bother you, but I don't have money for a payphone to call home."

The young black woman looked me over, seeming to feel sorry for me. "My phone is in the back. Follow me and I'll go get it for you."

She stepped away from the counter then told me to wait by the door that read EMPLOYEE ENTRANCE. I waited and looked around at the frozen food section that made me lick my lips. My stomach was still queasy, though, and for whatever reason, my eyes shifted to the row of feminine products, particularly a pregnancy test. I walked over to it and picked it up. Just to be sure, I slipped it into my back pocket and continued to wait for the young lady to bring me her phone. Minutes later, she came out of the door and gave the phone to me.

"I need to get back to my register, but once you're done with my phone, you can bring it to me."

"Thank you so much," I said. "I only need to make one call."

The chick went back to her register, and needing to keep her phone so badly, I stayed away from her register, then snuck by her and walked out the door. I needed some privacy first, so I made a quick turn down an alley and stood behind a Dumpster. I opened the box with the pregnancy test in it and dropped my jeans to pee on the stick.

Still feeling queasy and nervous at the same time, my eyes filled with water when I saw the results. I threw the stick on the ground, along with the box, and hurried to pull up my jeans. I was so emotional when I punched in Honey's cell phone number, and I was thankful that he answered.

"Honey, I need you right now," I cried. "I need for you to come get me before—"

The call dropped. That was what I'd thought, but then I realized that he'd hung up on me. I called back twice before he answered again.

"Karrine, I don't give a fuck what you need! Don't—"

"Please don't hang up!" I shouted while wiping the snot and tears that were pouring over my trembling lips. "I'm so sorry, and you have to believe me when I say that to you! Just come get me, please. I need you!"

I wiped my face and waited for him to speak, because there was silence.

"Honey, please! I don't know what I've gotten myself into, and I never meant to hurt anyone. Who . . . who did I kill? Tell me, because I am so, so sorry."

"Where in the fuck are you?"

I told Honey where I was and he ended the call. For now, all I could do was pace the alley, hoping that he would come soon.

For the next forty-five minutes, I kept going to the end of the alley, looking in both directions. The chick's phone that I'd had kept ringing, but none of the numbers were coming from Honey's phone, so I didn't bother to answer. I suspected it was her, calling to see where I had gone to with her phone. I'd thought about calling Chyna, too, but I wanted to talk to Honey first.

I walked back down the alley, holding my stomach and thinking about being pregnant. This was just too damn much. And what if I had killed the father of my damn child? I was becoming more and more like Mama every day, and I hated it. I didn't know what I was going to do with this child, and Lord knows the chaos that this shit would bring about.

As I was in thought, I heard screeching tires and quickly turned around. Honey's SUV was speeding down the alley, and when he spotted me from a distance, he slammed on the brakes. I was nervous as fuck when I saw him hurry out of the truck and slam the door. His locs were tied back and covered with a bandana, and the jeans he rocked hung low on his waist. The tank shirt he wore showed the muscles in his arms, and I'd be lying if I said I wasn't moved by his sexiness. Even the mean stare locked on his face could do him no harm, and when he rushed up to me, I couldn't believe that the first thing he did was slap the shit out of me with the back of his hand. The blow was so hard that I dropped down to one knee. He stood over me and gripped the back of my neck while squeezing it. He then pulled me up to look at him. I could taste blood stirring in my mouth, and I licked blood from my cracked lip.

"Bitch, how dare you fucking call me for help after what you did? You think I'm some silly muthafucka you can keep toying with? Is that what you think?"

I wanted to speak up, but Honey dragged me to the passenger's side of his truck and opened the door. He slammed my head on the seat, and as I was bent over, he stood behind me. He brought forth his gun and pressed the cold tip of it against my temple.

"You wanted me dead, but guess what? I want you dead, too. So does your mother, and you know damn well how I like to give her what she wants."

Tears soaked my face as he put pressure on my head, holding it down. Maybe him killing me wouldn't be such a bad thing after all, but I surely didn't want to go out like this.

"I'm so . . . sorry," I said very choked up. "I . . . I made a mistake, Honey, and I'm askin' for your forgiveness."

"A mistake?" he said, adding more pressure to my head that he was trying to flatten like a pancake. The pressure made my head feel like my brain was about to bust, and

I could barely breathe. "You didn't make no goddamn mistake! What you did was fuck up, bitch, you fucked up!"

"I know," I agreed, accepting his words. "And if you want to kill me, go right ahead and do it. Just know that you'll be killin' your child too."

Honey shouted out with laughter. "Is that all you got," he said. "Come up with something better, Karrine. You are so damn full of shit!"

Honey cocked the gun and my eyes grew wide. Damn, didn't this nigga hear what I'd just said.

"The Dumpster!" I shouted. "Go over to the Dumpster and look on the ground for the pregnancy test! You'll see it over there, and if you want me to, I'll take it again!"

Honey hesitated, but he released the gun from my temple. The pressure was lifted from my head and he backed inches away from me. "Stay right there. If you move, that's gon' be it for you."

I didn't dare move, and kept my head rested on the seat until he came back over to me, which was a few minutes later.

"Stand up and take your jeans off."

I stood up and saw that he had the other pregnancy test in his hand. There were two tests in the box and he gave the stick to me. "Pee on this. Now!"

I took the stick from his hand and pulled down my jeans. I had just peed, so it took me awhile to do it again.

"Hurry the fuck up," Honey shouted. "I don't have all goddamn day!"

The tone of his voice made me nervous. I strained, and it was enough to release enough pee on the stick. I gave it to him without even looking at it then pulled my jeans back up.

With a frown on his face, Honey glared at the stick then tossed it to the side. "Get in the fucking car and shut the door," he said.

I did as I was told, and he got in on the driver's side, slamming the door again.

"Why the fuck you ain't on no pills?" he asked.

"Because I'm not sexually active, and the only person I've had sex with for the past several years is you."

Honey released a deep sigh and shook his head. "Damn, Karrine," he yelled then slammed his hand on the steering wheel. "You know you killed my boy, BJ, don't you? That nigga protected me, and his family trusted me. I had to go to them . . . go to his muthafuckin' kids and family, and tell them a lie about somebody breaking into my crib and doing that shit to him. You put me in a fucked up situation. And why in the fuck would you try to kill me? I can't believe that you would try to kill me, of all people!"

I defended my actions. "But you tried to kill me too, didn't you?"

Honey hit the steering wheel again. "I told you that if I wanted to kill you, you'd be dead. But you damn sure wanted to kill me with that silencer you used, and the sad thing is, I'm so fucked up in the head right now that I don't know why I'm even sitting in this goddamn truck talking to the enemy."

"I'm far from bein' your enemy, but I'll let you figure out why you're here. In the meantime, I was fucked up in the head too, and I wanted to pay you back for what you'd done to me. I was also upset that after spillin' my guts to you about how I felt about you, you didn't say shit. You left me to assume that you didn't give a fuck about me, and the only thing I was to you was some ass. Whether you want to believe it or not, it's because of you that my life is so complicated. I wanted to put this thing between us to rest, but I now know that that was a stupid thing to do. I can't say I'm sorry enough about your friend, and whatever I can do to make things right with that situation, I will. Even if it means turnin' myself in to the police, just so his family can have peace."

Honey was thinking, hard. He kept sucking his teeth and looking over at me rolling his eyes. I saw them shift to my stomach, and that was when he released another sigh.

"First of all, if you know anything about me, Karrine, you know that I don't go around sharing my feelings and playing the fucking love game. It ain't me, so I don't know what the hell you were expecting."

"All I wanted you to say was that you cared for me too. You act like I wanted you to propose or something, but I didn't. I just needed to hear you say something, and unfortunately, your dick was just not enough, especially when you're known for spreadin' it real thin."

"You already know I care for you, so bump that shit. I'm not buying it, and you can't force me to say things to you that I'm not prepared to say. On another note, it ain't safe for you to come home with me right now. The door ain't open to you at Mama's house either. You need to chill somewhere, until I can figure out what it is that I need to do with you."

"If you don't think I should turn myself in to the police, all I need is some money and I'll get out of your way. I know you hate me right now, and I hate myself too for doin' all of this stupid stuff that has led me to this."

"Stop all that damn sobbing and foolish talk about the police because it ain't gon' do you no good. I have no sympathy for you, and just so you know, yo' ass ain't going nowhere until we decide what to do with our baby. If you run again, Karrine, you gon' wish I don't find you."

I sat, silent, as Honey drove to a nearby hotel and parked his truck. He told me to sit tight, and I did until he came back. I got out of the car and followed him into a hotel room that I was so delighted to see. All I wanted to do was take a hot bath and get some rest. After that, I guess we'd figure the other stuff out later.

"Stay here until I come back. I don't know how long that will be, so you gon' have to sit tight for a while. If you need me, you know the number."

I nodded, but called his name on his way out the door. He turned around, still frowning and looking mad as ever.

"Thank you. And I know that I'm in no position to ask you for anything, but I need a couple of favors before you go."

"You're out of favors, Karrine. Don't you know that?"

"I do, but this is important. Somebody is stalkin' Simone and I need for you to find out who it is and deal with him." I dug in my pocket and gave Honey the info I had written on the piece of paper. I wanted to deal with the situation myself, but with all that had happened, I couldn't do a thing. "That's his information. He knows where we live and Simone believes that he's been watchin' all of us. She doesn't want to tell Mama, and as you can see, my hands are tied."

Honey snatched the piece of paper from my hand and looked at it. He then put it inside of his pocket and folded his arms. "What else?" he asked.

"There's a lady named Patricia Simmons who lives in the shelter on Nineteenth Street. She has two children and they need help really bad. I was wonderin' if you would go in there and give her some money, and then offer her a place to stay in one of your rental properties. Just tell her that Karrine sent you, and she'll know who I am."

"I'm not doing no shit like that. And nobody stays in my shit for free."

"Please, Honey. I'll pay you back every last dime. I'll even somehow pay the place you rent to her, just do that for me, okay? It doesn't have to be no place spectacular, maybe one of your apartments with a few bedrooms and a nice kitchen. I've never asked you for anything, and this is so very important to me."

I found a piece of paper on the desk in the hotel room and wrote the name of the shelter and the lady's name on the paper, so he wouldn't forget. "Here," I said, reaching out to give the paper to him. He hesitated again, but snatched the paper from my hand.

"You know I have bigger things to worry about than this, don't you?" he griped.

"I know you do, and I just added another little headache to your list, didn't I? But before you go, just know this. Again, I apologize for what I've done, but I do love you, Honey. I love you even more now, but I don't have to tell you why. Now go take care of whatever it is that you need to take care of, and I'll be right here whenever you get back."

It was so obvious that Honey was fighting his feelings for me too. He walked to the door, and without turning around, he spoke up.

"The kind of love you're offering, I don't want it. Waste your time with someone else, not with me. We'll talk about the baby soon."

He left, but that was all Mama talking, not him. I, too, was wondering how she was going to feel about this, if she ever really found out.

# SIMONE

# 3

My stalker was starting to sound like a big-ass punk, who was all talk through messages and no action. I had started to fuck with him and respond to some of his messages. That seemed to make him more mad, and all he kept saying was that he couldn't wait until I left the house. I still hadn't gone anywhere, only because I didn't want to take any chances.

Meanwhile, things had quieted down around here. Mama seemed more at ease, but she was gone a lot, more than she was at home. Me and Chyna had the house to ourselves, but I sure did miss Karrine around here. I hadn't heard from her in a while, and it broke my damn heart. I kept asking Mama and Chyna if they'd heard from her, but none of them had either. I even left a voice mail message on Honey's phone, but he never did call me back. But as I was sitting at the kitchen table with Chyna, eating some Chinese food, my phone rang and it was him. His words caught me off guard.

"If you don't tell Mama what's going on, I will. You have less than an hour to do it."

"Huh?" I asked. "Excuse me, but what are you talkin' about?"

"I'm talking about the person who is stalking you. If you know or suspect who it is, you need to say something now before it's too late."

I pursed my lips. "So Karrine told you about this, right? Where is she anyway?"

"She's in good hands and you need not worry about her. What you need to do is worry about your stalker, because he's serious about doing something to you."

"Yeah, whatever. Bye Honey. Tell Karrine I said hello, but please let her know that I'm goin' to get in her shit about sharin' my business with you."

Honey ended the call and Chyna looked across the table at me. I hadn't said anything to her either, because I wasn't trying to make this a big deal. At the time when I spoke to Karrine, my stalker had just sent me a message and I was bothered by it. That was the only reason I had said something to her.

"Who was that?" Chyna asked.

"Honey. I called him to see if he knew where Karrine was, and he said that she was in good hands."

Chyna shrugged her shoulders. "Aw, okay. I finally talked to her earlier, and she said she was in a hotel room, chillin'. There's been a lot goin' on, and she mentioned somethin' else very interestin' to me. I made a promise to keep my mouth shut about it, though."

"Oooo, I want to know. Tell me what it is and I promise I won't say nothin'."

Chyna was trying to keep what she had known a secret, but when I kept asking her over and over again, she finally broke the news to me about Karrine being pregnant.

"What?" I shouted. "I'm so excited! Does Mama know?"

Chyna nodded and placed her finger in front of her lips. "Shhh, no she doesn't," Chyna whispered. "I'm sure Honey will tell her, or if not, Karrine. It ain't my place and it ain't yours either."

I frowned and reneged on my thoughts about being happy. "Honey? She pregnant by Honey?"

Chyna nodded and I couldn't believe what she was saying. Now where in the fuck do they do that at? This was all messed up, and I was downright confused.

"Yeah, they will have to be the ones to tell Mama about that, because I ain't touchin' it. I got enough on my plate already, and I've been trippin' so much that my clientele is slippin'. Last night was not a good night for me. I just couldn't get with it."

"It was a damn good night for me, only because I don't let all of this stuff get to me. You have to remember that business is business, and it doesn't need to be mixed with the personal shit you got goin' on. All you got to do is just keep on smilin' and pretendin' that everything is all good. None of those niggas will ever know that it ain't, and they don't pay to see you down in the dumps. They pay for you to be able to lift their spirits, so remember that."

I nodded, knowing that what Chyna said made sense. But she just didn't know what was going on with my stalker. Five minutes into our little chat, Mama came downstairs and interrupted us.

"Honey is on his way over here to talk to me about something. I don't want neither of y'all to say shit to him, and I'm not up for a bunch of arguing and carrying on today. I got a headache, and my goddamn blood pressure is up from y'all stressing me."

"No," Chyna teased. "Your blood pressure is up because you're not eatin' right, Mother. You had Chinese food, pizza, and barbecue last week, didn't you? And I'm not even goin' to count the sodas, because you've been getting' those in too."

Chyna and Mama kept going back and forth with each other, talking about high blood pressure and food. Since Honey was coming over, I suspected that he would tell Mama what was up with my stalker, so I had better open my mouth and say something before he did.

"Mama," I said, interrupting her conversation with Chyna. "I think I got a little problem that I need you to help me with."

She threw her hand back. "If it's your problem then it doesn't make it mine. Deal with it. I'm going to the casino after Honey leaves here, and I need to go upstairs to get dressed."

She turned and walked out of the kitchen. Well, at least she couldn't be mad at me for not telling her when I'd tried to. Chyna was interested in what my problem was, but by the time I could tell her, Honey was already at the door. Our last encounter didn't go over too well, so it wasn't like I appreciated being in his presence. To know that him and Karrine had been fucking around had me tripping and I had so many questions for her, as well as him. But those questions wouldn't get answered today because I was sure I'd have to deal with the backlash of keeping my stalker a secret.

Mama opened the front door, and Honey walked inside tall, dark, and fine as fuck. I couldn't blame Karrine for jumping on him, and if the motherfucker wasn't my for-real brother, I probably would be trying to get some too. I still didn't like his ass, and neither did Chyna. Mama did, though. She was all smiles when he came in. Her whole attitude had changed.

"Come on in the living room and have a seat," she said to Honey. "Do you want me to get you anything?"

"Nah, I'm good." He tossed his head back at me and Chyna. "What's up?" he said. "And y'all need to come on in here so I can holla at y'all too."

My stomach started to tighten. I knew what this would be about. Chyna had not a clue, so she went into the living room and sat on the couch. From the way Honey was looking, maybe this was something about Karrine. Was she okay? Now, I was starting to feel nervous and this little family gathering made me sweat.

I sat next to Chyna on the couch and Mama sat in a chair across from us. Honey leaned forward in the chair and rubbed his hands together.

"Normally, I stay out of other people's business," he said. "But here's the deal. A nigga named Blake has been stalking Simone, and he's real serious about taking action. I've had one of my boys on him for a few days, and he said the nigga is acting real crazy. He knows that

Blake has been casing the house several times during the day, and he's been driving by at night, too. I refuse to call the police to handle this, and I don't want to get nobody in this house in trouble either, because I'm sure this would be the first place the police come if we go to that nigga's crib and start tripping. Apparently he has plenty of photos of Simone, and a bunch of other shit too. So we need to get at him on our turf. Kind of catch him in the action then move like we do. After that, I suggest y'all shut that video porn shit down for a while and chill."

I looked at Mama and Chyna. They appeared shocked by what Honey had said. When Mama turned to me, I played clueless. "Two questions," she said. "Why is this muthafucka after you, and did you have any idea this shit was going on?"

I scratched my head and fidgeted. "I . . . uh, I was goin' to tell you earlier, but you said that my problems were mine and they weren't yours. And I don't know why he's after me. He just started sending me messages, buggin' me."

Honey quickly spoke up. "He's after Simone because she did the same shit they did to me, to him. She stole his money, racked up on his credit card bills then threatened him not to go to the police."

I looked at Honey and rolled my eyes. "Why you gotta be such a muthafuckin' hater and snitch? Damn, nigga, don't you know when to keep yo' mouth shut?"

Honey kept at it. "She's known about her stalker for a while now, and she has also known that he knows all of us by first and last names."

I could feel all hell about to break loose. When Mama rushed out of the chair and charged at me, all I could do was crouch down and cover my face.

"You! Stupid! Fucking! Bitch!" she said, pounding the back of my head with her tightened fists. "Why in the fuck didn't you say nothing? Why, Simone? You could have gotten all of us killed!"

Her fists were now pounding into my back. I had kneeled on the floor just so I wouldn't eventually land there.

"Get yo' ass up!" Mama yelled. I surely didn't want to, but I feared that she would start kicking the shit out of me. I slowly stood up, seeing that Honey and Chyna had moved out of the way. Mama's chest was heaving in and out and she could barely catch her breath. She pointed her finger in my face and dotted my face with spit sprinkles as she shouted at me.

"I can't believe that all this time, you allowed me, Chyna, and Karrine to walk out of this house, knowing that a crazy son of a bitch could have been waiting out there to kill us! No wonder yo' ass ain't been nowhere, you scary bitch! Spare your fucking life, but to hell with us!"

I kept blinking as her hands were waving in my face. When she paused from talking, she slapped the shit out of me and grabbed the back of my hair, yanking the shit out of my head. I tried to hold back my tears, but when several of them fell down my face, I hurried to smack them away with my hand.

"I was scared, Mama," I yelled. "That's why I didn't say nothin'! His messages made me scared and I didn't know what to do!"

Mama pulled my head back like she was a pitcher in the major baseball league getting ready to throw a ball. With all of her power, she flung my head forward and let go. I staggered and crashed to the floor, almost banging my head on the edge of the glass table. Like a madwoman, Mama stood over me and spoke through gritted teeth.

"I tell you what yo' ass gon' do. You gon' stand yo' ass outside until that nigga shows up again. If he fires some bullets into yo' ass, so damn what! That's what you get for fucking with him. Face your fears and confront a nigga when you done fucked him over. You had no business doin' what you did, and I should beat yo' trifling ass for bringing this shit to my doorstep!"

I was shaking all over. When I looked up and saw the smirk on Honey's face, that shit pissed me off. An angry look washed over Chyna's face, but I don't know who she was mad at—me or Mama.

I couldn't express my anger to Mama because I knew I'd get fucked up. What I did, though, was turn this shit back on Honey. He had fucked himself by coming here and snitching on me. And I was going to make him wish that he hadn't done that.

As Mama continued to rant, I stared at Honey with fire in my eyes. "You bastard," I hissed. "I hate yo' fuckin' guts!"

Mama would surely take up for him, and that was what she had done. "You leave him out of this, bitch, and watch yo' damn mouth. He the only half decent child I got, and you hoes be straight-up trippin'!"

"Decent?" I fired back at Mama. "How you gon' consider an asshole who fucked yo' damn daughter and got her pregnant decent? Ain't he like her damn brother? I don't give a shit if he step or not, you still both of they Mamas!"

Now the nigga jumped bad and decided to speak up. "Shut the fuck up, Simone. You wasn't saying all that shit when you was riding my dick in that hotel room. Don't be trying to switch the subject around here. After all, this is really about you, not about me and Karrine."

Chyna wasn't saying nothing. Like me, she knew the shit was gone hit the fan, especially when Mama's eyes had focus on Honey with daggers in them.

"What is she talking about, Honey? Is there something else that I need to know?"

He hesitated to speak then released one word. "No."

Mama's face twisted and her forehead was stacked with thick, sweaty wrinkles. "No what, nigga? Is Karrine pregnant?"

I got my ass off the floor so I could see this shit go down. And when Honey didn't answer, I answered for him. "Yes, she is pregnant. Tell her, Honey. Go ahead and tell her the truth!"

Mama caught me tripping when she swung her hand around and slapped the fuck out of me again. I'd just about had it with this shit and I tightened my fists. I took a few steps forward and was ready to fuck Mama up.

"Come on, bitch," Mama said with tightened fists, too. "I dare you, just so I can have a reason to knock yo' ass out cold!"

This time, Chyna ran over and stood between us. "Stop this, please!" she yelled. "Why are y'all doin' this? Damn!"

"Chyna, move yo' ass out of the way."

Mama shoved Chyna to the side and she crashed into the wall. She also looked like she wanted some action.

Honey got Mama's attention when he opened his mouth. "Yes, she is pregnant," he said. "But we're not sure if we gon' keep the baby."

Mama stared at him without a single blink. "Did you not listen to what I told you, Honey? I told you that Karrine was off limits, didn't I?"

"Of course you did, but I'm a grown man, she's a grown woman, and we make our own decisions."

That was not the correct thing to say to Mama, and that grown shit didn't fly. "Grown," she laughed. "Nigga, I'ma show you grown. Stay right there and I'ma go get it for you."

Honey was ready to make a move, and so were me and Chyna. We knew that Mama had run off to get her gun, but I heard her in my bedroom, slamming things around. It sounded as if she had crashed my computer, and through her ranting words, I knew that was what she had done.

"Tell her to holla at me when she calms down," Honey said, looking at Chyna. He got the fuck out of there, and by the time Mama had rushed down the stairs, Honey was already in his truck, getting ready to back out of the driveway. He hurried to start his truck, but Mama fired several shots from her Glock that blew bullets into the side of his truck.

The pinging sound of the bullets hitting his truck was sounding off like firecrackers. His tires screeched, causing smoke to arise as he burned rubber. I couldn't believe that Mama kept on firing, and we kept screaming her name, but she wouldn't listen.

Then, all of a sudden, something strange happened. A car traveling extremely fast started coming down the street. We all paused to look at the speeding car, but none of us had seen it before. Mama lowered her gun, but seconds later, several bullets sprayed from the car, causing every last one of us to run for cover. All I could hear were the echoes of what sounded like a machine gun, spraying the front of our house with bullets. For what seemed like five long minutes, but was only several seconds, everything went blank. The car quickly sped away, but Chyna and me stood in shock as we looked at Mama on the ground with bullet holes in her chest. She squirmed around on the ground with blood dripping from the corner of her mouth.

"Maaaaama!" Chyna yelled, then ran up to her.

Honey rushed back and got out of his truck too, but he was limping as he came to her aid.

I just stood there in shock with tears streaming down my face. My whole body was shaking as if it were zero degrees outside. This couldn't be happening right now. It had to be a dream. Mama wasn't going to die because of me, was she? I knew the man in the car was Blake because I had seen his face. I wanted to kill him, and doing so would bring me much pleasure.

"Move back," Honey yelled, trying to pull Chyna away from Mama.

She, however, rocked Mama in her arms and pressed on the bullet wounds, trying to stop the rushing blood. "No, Mama, please don't die!" she cried out. "We need you, please!"

Honey had to drag Chyna away from Mama, just so he could pick up her limp body. "Stay the fuck out of the way!" he shouted. "I need to get her to the hospital!"

He glared at me as he carried Mama in his arms and put her into his truck. Chyna kept rushing up to him, pounding on him and telling him to put Mama down. "Where are you goin' with her? Leave her the fuck alone! Let her go!"

Honey pushed Chyna back with much force. She fell to the ground, and that was when he jumped in the truck and sped off. Chyna turned to me and yelled for me to go get the keys to my car. My body was still trembling all over, but I rushed inside to find my keys. When I got to my room, it was a mess. Mama had definitely crashed my computer, and my whole desk had been tilted over. I searched for my keys, but couldn't find them. Five minutes later, Chyna ran into the house, yelling at me.

"What in the fuck is takin' you so long? Damn! We need to get to the hospital!"

"I can't find my keys in all of this mess! Go get your keys so we can go!"

Chyna got her keys and we rushed out of the house together, closing the door but not locking it. Both of us were sobbing in the car, and I looked over at Chyna who, before, I had rarely seen shed one tear.

"I'm sorry," I said. "I know this is all my fault, but I had no idea nothin' like this would happen."

Chyna said not one word on the way to the hospital. All she did was gaze straight ahead. I kept my mouth shut too, but when we arrived at the hospital, there was no sign of Honey's truck. Still, we got out of the car and ran through the emergency room entrance. With bloodstains covering her clothes, Chyna rushed up and down the hallway, asking the check-in nurses at the desk if Mama had been recently brought in.

"No," the nurse behind the desk said. "But calm down. Let me see if I can help you ladies."

We stood in a panic as the nurse made several calls, but she didn't have any luck.

"I'm sorry," she said. "We haven't had anyone check in by that name."

"Then where in the fuck are they?" Chyna yelled.

She reached in her pocket to get her cell phone. She punched in Honey's number, but the call went straight to voice mail.

"See, this nigga playin' with me," she said, rushing out of the hospital.

We both looked around, but no Mama. No Honey. Chyna started to cry harder. She fell to her knees and pounded on the ground.

"Where are they?" she cried out. "I knew I shouldn't have let that muthafucka take her! I knew it!"

I was so speechless. If there was ever a time in my life that I had wanted to kill myself, this was surely it.

"Let's go to his house," I said. "I know where he lives, don't you? If not, Karrine does. We can call her and maybe she knows where he is."

Chyna slowly got off the ground and all I wanted to do was hug her, but I couldn't. I knew she had to be mad at me, and this wasn't a good feeling.

We got into the car, and when we drove to Honey's house the inside was pitch black. We still knocked on the door, but got no answer. Called his phone again . . . no answer. Not having any luck, Chyna drove to a hotel. She said that Karrine had been living there, so we both went inside and Chyna went straight to her room.

A few minutes later, Karrine opened the door and stared at both of us with devastating looks on our faces. Her eyes widened as she looked at the blood on Chyna's clothes and at the tears that just kept on flowing. Without even knowing what was up, tears rushed to the rim of Karrine's eyes.

"Wha . . . what's going on? Ple . . . please don't tell me somethin' bad has happened."

We said nothing, until Karrine widened the door and we walked in. Chyna reached out to grab Karrine around the neck and held her tight with staggering breaths.

"Mama was shot. We . . . we don't know if she's dead or alive because Honey took her."

Karrine backed away from Chyna and her face turned as white as snow. She shook her head from side to side and scratched at her chest. "Is . . . is she dead?" Karrine questioned.

"We don't know. We don't fuckin' know, but there ain't no damn way she'll survive somethin' like that."

"What happened?" Karrine had so much pain in her eyes.

Chyna started to tell her about how everything went down, including me and Mama's argument. All I could do was stagger away from them. I cried out and dropped to my knees. More snot ran from my nose, and as my head was slumped near the floor, I began to pull my hair. I hated my fucking self, and it was my fault that my family was going through this. This shit was all on me, and I should have said something a long time ago about Blake. I shouldn't have robbed his ass either, and shame on me for not thinking that this shit wouldn't come back to haunt me.

As I lay on the floor losing it, I felt a hand on my back. "I can't even say if it's gon' be okay or not, but don't feel bad, Simone. We will always have each other, and what we got to do is stick together, no matter what."

The sound of Karrine's voice did me no good. Like a madwoman, I pulled out every strand of weave in my hair and rolled on my back, gagging. No matter how Karrine was looking at this, I had fucked up. Mama was dead, all because of me. At this point, I wanted to die too.

## *CHYNA*

# 4

Life wasn't the same without Mama around and so many things had changed. It had been six months ago since the incident in front of the house had taken place and the truth was that we still didn't know if she was dead or alive. She had simply disappeared, and so had Honey. I don't care how many times we had driven to his house to see if we could catch up with him, there was no sign of him. The only person who came to the door was that white chick Trice. I know she got sick of us stopping by, and it basically did us no good because she wasn't upping any information. After a while, we stopped going by there. I figured if Mama wanted us to know that she was alive and well, she would tell us. It was as if she was really dead, though, and it was so hard for all of us to cope.

The video porn business was a wrap. I, eventually, started doing hair four days a week, and I had moved into the apartment that I had already had on a permanent basis. Karrine was still living at the hotel, and her tab had been covered for quite some time. She had a part-time job at a clothing store, selling shoes. She was into the fashion thing, so that job was right up her alley. She was still with child, so she'd found a job that wouldn't put too much stress on her.

As for Simone, she had gone back to school, and she was working at Wal-Mart. It took me awhile to forgive my sister for withholding information about Blake, but I realized that anyone of us could have been put in that predicament. I couldn't say that I would have said anything about a stalker either, but it was surely a decision that all of us regretted. Not only that, but we'd had regrets about so many other things too. I could go on and on about how we needed to get our shit together, but we had failed to do it. Our wakeup calls had come too late, so now we had to deal with the fact that Mama was gone, we didn't know if Blake was still around or not, and Karrine would have to raise a child all by herself. Simone said that Blake had stopped messaging her, though, so that was good news. I certainly couldn't pinpoint why he'd stopped, but it did make me more comfortable, going around and doing things.

On Friday evenings, me, Karrine, and Simone always met for dinner at Applebee's. Now that everyone was living separately, we made it our business to meet up and chat. While we still talked to each other every single day, I looked forward to when Friday's came so I could see my sisters. As always, I was the first one there. I sat at a booth, sipping on lemon water until I saw Karrine enter with her big ole belly. She looked so adorable pregnant, and Honey had no idea what he was missing. As she wobbled up to the table, I stood to give her a hug.

"Awww," I said. "Don't you look too cute in your new maternity outfit."

"Cute wouldn't be the word to describe me. I look like a fat pig and don't you see how big my nose is gettin'?" She wiggled her nose. "Look at it."

I laughed and shook my head. Karrine sat down and seconds later, Simone came in. I waved my hand so she could see us. She was still a diva and removed her shades as she headed our way. Her tight leather pants hugged her hips and the heels she wore made her extremely tall.

"Look at you, hooker," I teased. "Where is your stripper pole at?"

"It's at my man's house. Waitin' for me to swing on it again."

We laughed and sat down to get the scoop on Simone's new man she was telling us about. He was one of her professors at school and she seemed intrigued by him.

"He's so smart," she said. "And y'all already know I love me a smart man."

"I guess," I said, folding my arms. "As long as he got street smarts too. It don't make sense to have book smarts and no street smarts."

"I agree," Karrine said. "I'll take a street smart nigga any day, over a book smart one."

Simone disagreed, but we picked up our conversation, after we ordered our food.

"No word from Honey yet?" I asked Karrine. "Not one single word, but he did take care of that lady at the shelter I told y'all about. I gave up on leavin' him messages, and the funny thing is I don't know if I'm angry about all of this or not. He and Mama have to be somewhere together. I truly believe that they are, and shame on them for not callin' and sayin' anything."

"I know," I said. "But then again, maybe he's so upset with us that he don't want anything else to do with us. Maybe she died and he just said to hell with us. That could be the case too."

"I don't know what to think," Simone said. "I've thought about it over and over again, but I don't want to give up hope. I keep thinkin' that one day Mama is goin' to walk through somebody's door and say . . . bitches, I'm home! Get y'all muthafuckin' asses up and clean my house!"

We all laughed.

"Right," I said. "I miss her so much, and I just want one last chance to tell her how sorry I am for not understanding who she really was. We just didn't have the average Mama y'all, but there was somethin' so unique about Taffy Douglas that was very loving. No matter what, neither of us can deny that she always had our backs and then some. That woman loved us, and it's so funny that I didn't really see that shit until later."

Karrine wiped several tears that ran down her face. "I know. And I feel so bad for the way I acted. I betrayed her time and time again, and now I have to live with that shit. The last time I saw her keeps playin' in my head and I keep rememberin' all the harsh shit I'd said."

"Me too," Simone added. "I keep thinkin' about that day in the livin' room. For the first time, I was about to hit her back. I hate talkin' about this shit, because it is so damn tragic how you just don't realize a good damn thing until it's gone."

"Well, I'ma keep hope alive," I said then picked up my glass of water. So did Simone and Karrine and we held them up together. "Here's to Mama. Wherever she is, may she get some peace, yet know that these bitches right here will forever love her."

"Amen," Simone said. "Don't know love or show love, unless it's for the love of our family."

We drank to that and continued our sister-love dinner at Applebee's.

# *TAFFY*

# 5

Yeah, them bitches found out that I was alive and doing well, but not until after Karrine had the baby. There was no way that I was going to keep Honey away from his child, and I wasn't going to stay away from my grandbaby either.

That didn't mean that I wouldn't stay away from my daughters, because I had not spoken to anyone, and they still didn't know my whereabouts. I was far, far away from home, taking in the beautiful sun and the white sandy beaches. I spent most of my time by the poolside, sipping on Gin and a little juice, having the time of my life.

That's right . . . my life. A life that had been put on the backburner for too long because I refused to let go of my daughters. The problem was, them motherfuckers had to learn how to grow up. They had to learn responsibilities, and the only way they would learn to handle their own shit was if I wasn't around. I still knew exactly what they'd been up to, and while they made nowhere near as much money as they had made from doing video porn, they was learning how to survive in a way that wasn't so confrontational. That was fine with me, and it didn't bother me not one bit that I was here, and they were there.

I was waiting by the poolside with my straw hat and a black sexy swimsuit on, my Prada glasses shielding my eyes from the sun. Honey was supposed to be here about an hour ago with my grandbaby, but he was late. When Karrine learned that I was alive, she wanted to speak to me, but I refused. All I wanted was to spend time with my grandbaby, and Karrine allowed that to happen.

I didn't ask much about her and Honey's relationship, but I knew that there wasn't much going on with it, because Honey was spending most of his time at this house with me. There was too damn much going on in Chicago, especially after Honey murdered Blake, and we both thought it would be best for us to handle business from here. Honey remained the wonderful, loving, loyal, intelligent, sexy—y'all get the picture—son who would do just about anything for me. I was glad that I hadn't killed his ass that day. He'd saved my life, and if it wasn't for his prompt actions, I would be dead.

The funny thing about that day was that when I had gone into my room to get my gun, I eased a bulletproof vest underneath my dress. I knew that Honey had a gun in his car, and I was so sure that he was going to fire it at me when I shot at him. But even in a moment like that, he didn't turn on me. Not once, even when he was a little boy, did he turn on me like his father had done. Honey stuck by me through thick and thin, and that nigga walked through the fire with me. My girls just didn't understand what walking through the fire with somebody meant, yet.

Even when it came to Karrine, Honey didn't turn on her, either. He may have taken care of her from afar, but he still took care of her every need. The bottom line was that he loved Karrine and I knew it. I could see it in his eyes, but he remained loyal to me. He knew that I would never accept the two of them getting married or anything like that. The baby was enough, and I understood that the two of them needed to get their fuck on every once in a while.

"It's about damn time," I said, putting my drink with an umbrella in it on the table next to me. I reached out for my grandbaby, Shania, who was gorgeous, just like me. She was so adorable, and I couldn't wait to kiss her fat, sweet cheeks.

Honey sat her in my lap, and at five months old, she damn sure knew who her grandmother was. A huge smile was on her face as she looked into my bright eyes. "Hello, my beautiful little girl," I said, kissing those cheeks. "Muuuuah!"

I held her close to my chest and squeezed her. "What took you so doggone long?" I griped to Honey. "I've been sitting here waiting and waiting on you to get back here."

Honey sat on the lounging chair next to me, squinting from the sun. "I had to make several stops. Shania wanted to get you something real special for your birthday, and she hopes you like it."

"My birthday," I said, cocking my head back. "Is it really my birthday?"

Honey nodded.

"Damn, I must've forgotten. How old am I today?"

"Fifty-three, so stop pretending that you're that old and can't remember nothing."

I shrugged my shoulders and turned my attention back to my grandbaby. Honey got up, and a few minutes later, he came back with a birthday cake in his hands. He sat it on the table and lit one candle with his lighter. Honey started to sing "Happy Birthday" to me, but when I heard a few others join in, I snapped my head to the side. Karrine, Chyna, and Simone all had gifts in their hands and were coming down the steps in the backyard, heading my way.

"Aw, hell naw," I said, handing my grandbaby back over to Honey. "Y'all gon' make me show my ass in front of my grandbaby already. I did not invite these heifers over here."

Chyna was the first one to run up to me, giddy as ever. "Mamaaaa!" she shouted. "Stop bein' so doggone mean and give me a hug. Ain't you glad to see us?"

"Not really, but I guess I don't have a choice, since Honey around here doing shit that I told him not to do."

"I listen to you on some things, not all things," Honey said. "Besides, they twisted my arm behind my back and held a gun to my head. I really didn't have no other choice."

Simone and Karrine ran up to me too. Everybody was reaching out for hugs, but the only person who was getting a hug from me was Shania, who was back in my arms.

"Back away from us," I said, shooing the others away.

"Okay," Simone said. "I see how we get played, but it's all good. Happy birthday, old lady. At least give me a kiss."

Simone bent down and patted her cheek. Thinking about the last time I had seen her, and about what had happened, I couldn't help but to kiss her cheek.

"Ooo, she gets one and I can't even get a hug?" Chyna whined then pouted. "I see now who your favorite is."

"No," Karrine said with her hand on her hip. "We all know who her favorite is, and it damn sure ain't none of us."

They all looked at Honey and pointed to him. He laughed, then pointed to Shania. "Uh, no, not me. Her. Sorry."

I gave Shania a hug and stood up to greet my girls the correct way. I was very happy to see my Trouble Makin' Mamas, so I opened my arms. "Come on over here, bitches, and let me give y'all some love. Good seeing y'all, but please don't bring y'all asses back here unless y'all are invited."

They laughed, but you'd better believe I meant what the fuck I'd said. Period.

# KARRINE

# 6

I couldn't believe how much Mama had chilled. These days, my daughter, Shania, kept Mama busy. She spent more time with Mama than she did with me and Honey, but that was all good. The only problem was that Mama was now in California, but we were still in Chicago. I wanted to move there, but I preferred to give Mama all the space she said she needed. It also gave me, Chyna, and Simone a chance to live our own lives and do our own thing, without Mama running the show and telling us what to do. She still tried to throw in her input every now and then, especially since she and Honey remained very close. He'd been going back and forth from California to Chicago. Sometimes he'd be here for several weeks, and then he'd go back to California to handle his business with Mama.

Our relationship had gotten stronger, but we still had issues to deal with. After Shania was born, I decided that Honey was the nigga I would be down with forever. He took good care of me and Shania, and we didn't want for much. I still had concerns about his healthy sexual appetite, but I'd gotten to a point where I didn't trip off of Honey being with other bitches so much. As long as he didn't bring no bitch to our doorstep, he didn't give me any diseases, and he didn't put nobody else before me, I was good. That was what I had thought, until I listened to

Chyna tell me that she'd seen him with a pregnant chick yesterday.

"Chyna, you know that Honey knows a lot of people," I said while sitting on the bed, polishing my toenails. The phone was held up to my ear with my shoulder. "That bitch could have been anybody."

"She could have, but by the way they were lookin' at each other, somethin' was up. I'm just tellin' you this for your own good. Either you can look into it, or you don't have to. I've done my part."

"You know I appreciate it, and I'll deal with Honey soon."

"I hope so, and I must say that I'm still not feelin' this relationship between y'all. I think you can do much better. Just because you got a child by him doesn't mean you gotta stay with him."

"The truth is, I was in love with Honey way before Shania even got here. And he's not as bad as you and Simone make him out to be. I know y'all don't like him, but I think it has more to do with his close relationship with Mama. I've grown to accept it, but you and Simone haven't."

"I guess you could be right, so in order to keep the peace, I'ma just keep my mouth shut. On another note, where is my niece at? I barely get to spend any time with her and that's a damn shame."

"You already know where she's at. I'm goin' to Cali this weekend to go get her, because yo' Mama thinks she done had another baby."

"Yeah, I noticed that, but it's good to see Mama so relaxed now. She don't have to be all alone in that big-ole house, and Shania is just what she needed to calm herself down."

We both had to laugh about that. "I don't know if she's calmed down or not, but I do know that her and

Honey still be doin' some crooked shit. And while they're so busy with my baby, I'm the one stuck in this big ole house by myself. I'm thinkin' about lookin' for a job, just to keep myself busy when Honey ain't here. A bitch gets tired of shoppin', goin' to fancy restaurants, and spas. I'm kind of disappointed in my life right now."

"That's because you under Honey's spell. He wants you right there, doin' nothin', while that nigga run the streets and do whatever he wants to. Wake yo' ass up and start gettin' out more. Live a little, and if you want to do somethin' different, do it."

What Chyna said made sense. My entire life revolved around Honey, and it was time for a change. Chyna worked customer service at a beverage distributing company now, and said she would look into any openings for me. When I heard the front door open, I figured it was Honey coming home, so I told Chyna I would call her back. I put the phone down, then got out of bed and looked at myself in the floor mirror that sat in front of our king-sized bed. My gold silk robe hung off my shoulders. I looked at my naked body that was still flawless, but not as perfect as it was before the baby. My stomach was a little pudgy, so I thought about joining a gym to work some of that off. I pulled the robe together and tightened my belt. My short hair had been recently trimmed, but it was definitely time for me to redo my long, fake lashes. I straightened my arched brows and moistened my lips with lip gloss. I assumed Honey would have come to the bedroom by now, but he hadn't. It was eleven o'clock in the morning, and since he'd been out all night, I left the bedroom to go question him about what Chyna had told me.

I stood at the top of the stairs and watched as Honey went into his office and closed the door. He was on his cell phone, but I couldn't hear a word he was saying. All

I heard was laughter, and I was slightly taken aback that
he hadn't come to see what was up with me first. He knew
I had been here for the past few days by myself. I thought
he was in California, but according to Chyna, he wasn't.
Plus, I had only spoken to him twice in the past three
days. Honey had always made it his business to call me
three or four times a day. Something was definitely up.

Trying to show him some respect, I knocked on the
door before entering his office. When I walked in, he was
still on his cell phone, but he put his finger on his lips
as a gesture for me to be quiet. I sat on the couch and
crossed my legs. As I waited for him to end his business
call, I checked him out in his baggy jeans and red, V-neck
T-shirt that hugged his muscles. The tats on his strong
arms were on display, and the color red went well with
his smooth, dark chocolate complexion. The trimmed
hair on his chin made him look sexy as fuck! My pussy
already started to do a little dance for him, but before
that bitch got too excited, I had to find out what was up
with him and the pregnant chick.

Whoever Honey was talking to must've been working
his nerves, because he kept sighing and raising his brows.
His locs had grown past his shoulders, but he had them
pulled back into a ponytail. Seeing that I was getting
impatient with his phone call, he finally put it to an end.

"Get at me a li'l later about that shit," he said to the
caller. "Until then, hold it down and don't let that nigga
out of your sight."

Honey nodded, and a few seconds later, he laid his cell
phone on the desk.

"Sorry about that," he said. "I had to take care of a
problem that was brewing."

"No problem, but I have a little problem that's brewin',
too. Maybe you can help me resolve my issue as quickly
as possible."

Honey got up and came over to where I was. He bent down to give me a peck on the lips then he pulled me up from the couch so he could sit down and I could sit on his lap.

"Let's hear it," he said. "Tell me about this problem you have."

I looked him in the eyes, just so I could see if he would lie to me when I started to question him. "Where were you yesterday?" I asked.

His eyes remained connected with mine and didn't shift. "I was in California until early afternoon. I came here to take care of some business, but as you can see, it took me awhile to handle some things. I couldn't get here until now."

"You know I don't really get into all that shit you and Mama got goin' on behind closed doors, but I have a feelin' that this business you talkin' about ain't got nothin' to do with her. Am I wrong?"

This time, Honey's eyes shifted to the right then back at me. "You're right, but we don't need to get into this right now, do we? I haven't seen you in several days and I thought we could hang out tonight at the club. A friend of mine is having a party, so do you feel like going or what?"

"I'm not sure yet, because here's the deal. Chyna saw you with a pregnant bitch yesterday. Are you goin' to tell me what's up with that, or do I need to make some phone calls and find out who this chick is myself?"

Honey licked his lips and slowed his hands as they rubbed my thighs. "Her name is Shay. She's six months pregnant, but I don't know if the baby is mine or not. She say it is, but I know she been fucking with a lot of niggas who live on her block. All I did yesterday was meet up with her to see what was up."

I got off Honey's lap and walked away. Shania wasn't even a year old yet, and there he was, already making more babies. We had been trying to do this relationship thing for quite some time. I at least thought Honey would be smart enough to use condoms when he was out there fucking with these bitches, and if Shay had been with other niggas, why go up in that shit raw?

"I have so much that I could say to you right now, but I'm not goin' there with you," I said. "Since you decided to stroll up in here this mornin', I take it that you spent the night with her."

"I stayed at Maurice's crib, waiting on a drop to come. I was only with Shay for about an hour, if that."

I glared at Honey, then walked to the door and opened it. He wasn't about to get me to act a goddamn fool about this pregnant bitch, or about him not coming home and not calling me. My gut already told me something wasn't adding up, and I never trusted shit he said, especially not when I trusted my instincts more.

Thing is, situations like these were hard. Whenever you had a nigga who you knew loved you, who protected you, and who took care of your financial needs, this shit was difficult to walk away from. I couldn't always trip off everything that didn't add up, and, sometimes, I had to take Honey's word for shit, even though I didn't want to. I often found myself trying to pick and choose my battles with him. I didn't know if the child was his or not, so until I knew for sure, this wasn't a battle I was willing to have with him. I did take issue with the nigga going up in hoes without a condom on, but my solution to that problem was simple. If he didn't want to use one with them, he would have to use one with me.

Seething with anger that I had learned to hide very well, I went into the kitchen to get something to drink. I opened the fridge, and when I reached for the orange juice, I felt Honey standing behind me, pressing his dick against my ass. He planted a trail of soft kisses along my neck and wrapped his arms around my waist.

"I know you're upset with me, ma, but you ain't got no reason to be mad. Do you think my dick would really be this hard right now, if it was sitting pretty in another pussy all night? Come on, baby, you know better than that, don't you?"

I turned around to face Honey. His jeans were already unzipped, and I could see his hard dick stretching the fabric of his briefs, trying to escape. I reached down and carefully pulled his dick out so I could see it. I examined it first, making sure there was no leftover glaze to be seen. There wasn't, so I wrapped my hand around his meat and squeezed it.

Honey thought I was massaging it, until I added more pressure and locked his shit with a tight grip. His face twisted and he bit down on his lip.

"Fuck," he shouted and squeezed my wrist. As he pinched my skin, it caused me to grip his dick harder. "Let it go! Now!"

I held a smirk on my face and dealt with the pain of him pinching my wrist. In no way did it cause me more harm that what I was doing to him.

"The next time you stick this muthafucka in another bitch, wrap yo' shit up, nigga. If you give me any goddamn diseases, I swear I'm gon' cut this shit off and flush it down the damn toilet. Got it?"

By now, Honey was squeezing his eyes together, trying to pull away from me. When I let go of his dick, his eyes shot open. He held his dick and rubbed it. "Ahhhhh," he said, looking relieved.

As he soothed the pain with his hands, I inched away from him, then broke out running. I knew he was coming after me, I just wasn't sure if that was a good or bad thing.

By the time I reached the third step, Honey had caught up with me. He grabbed my ankle, but I kicked my feet, trying to keep him at a distance.

"Yo' ass ain't going nowhere," he said. "Come here!"

He yanked me down one step, but I swung my feet and karate kicked him right in the chin. That caused him to release my ankle, so I flew up a few more stairs before he grabbed my silk robe from the back, tearing it off me. This time, he grabbed both of my ankles, and I went crashing down at the top of the stairs. My knees burned from the carpet, and as I lay on my stomach, Honey stood over me. He removed his black leather belt that barely held up his sagging jeans. Making me pay for what I'd done to him, he slapped my ass with the belt real hard, causing it to sting.

"Ouch," I yelled out and covered my ass with my hand.

"You should have known better than to do some shit like that," he said. "Now that ass gon' have to pay, and you gon' need to put some for-real healing on my dick."

I tried to crawl away, but Honey dropped to his knees and straddled my back so I couldn't move.

"Get up," I strained to say. "You're too heavy."

"So. And I'm not getting up until you tell me you're sorry and that you love me."

I pursed my lips and dealt with the pain of Honey being on my back. He started to pounce on me, and when my back started to hurt more, I grunted out loudly.

"Say it," he said.

Still getting nothing out of me but grunts, he jumped up and quickly removed his jeans. Of course I wanted him to fuck me, but I continued to play hard to get. As I crawled a few inches away, he slapped my ass with the belt again.

"Would you stop that shit?" I said, frowning. "That damn belt hurts."

"You think I don't know that? It's supposed to hurt. Now you see how I felt. It's healing time, ma, so put up and shut up."

Honey pulled me back to the top of the stairs, and as he kneeled on the third step, he lifted me off my stomach and on my knees.

"Hike that ass in the air," he said. "I haven't tasted your pussy in several days, and I'm real hungry."

I bent far over, exposing my shaved, pretty slit to him. My clit poked through my slit, and as Honey balanced himself on the steps, he massaged my ass cheeks then pulled them far apart. I felt his fingers dip inside of me. He flickered them in a come here motion, and I could hear my pussy getting ready to clown. My head slumped and I shut my eyes.

"You wet enough," Honey said. "But I don't know if you want my dick first or my tongue action. Which one?"

Both were very satisfying, so either way, he couldn't go wrong. All I did was reach back and pull my right ass cheek further away from the left.

"It don't matter, baby. Just get in there, please."

Honey pulled out his fingers, bringing along a healthy amount of my juices that slowly trickled down my legs. I felt his thick tongue circle my clit, and then he slithered that sucker so far up in me that I started to rock my body against his face.

"Yo . . . you gon' make me cum," I said, curling my toes and squeezing my fist. His tongue flicked faster. "Daaamn, Honey, why you doin' this shit?"

His mouth was filled with good pussy, so he couldn't answer me. I rocked faster, but as I neared an orgasm, Honey released his tongue and filled me with his dick. I had already reneged on the deal with the condom, but I promised myself that this would be the last time he would enter me without it.

For the next several minutes, our bodies rocked perfectly together, even while in the awkward position that we were in on the steps. Honey turned me out, and he was so deep inside of me that his balls slapped my ass with a sweet kiss behind each thrust. I could barely catch my breath because of the fast pace, and the sweat from his forehead started to drip on me. My pussy was taking a severe beating, but I loved every single bit of it.

As I neared an orgasm, I told Honey what he wanted to hear. "I . . . I'm sorry for squeezin' this good dick, baby, and you know I loooove yo' black ass. Me and this pussy love the fuck out of you, and we hooked on you like a mutha!"

Honey gripped my hips and tightened his muscular ass as he released his excitement inside of me. He didn't dare move, but I did. I threw my ass back to him so fast that I almost made him fall back on the steps. So weak in the moment, he stumbled backward, but held on to the rail to catch himself from falling.

"You are determined to kill me, ain't you?" he said. This time, he slapped my ass with his hand and eased his limp, wet dick out of me. "Ahhhh, what a relief. You did good, ma, real good."

I turned around and sat on the top stair, facing him. "So did you, and even though I'm not mad at you anymore, would you please do me a favor?"

Honey moved forward to kiss me. "Anything. Right about now, you can ask me for anything."

"Would you please start usin' condoms from now on when we have sex? I know that dick of yours is nasty and I don't want no parts of it without a condom."

By the look in Honey's narrowed eyes, something told me to run. I did, but this time, he caught up with me in our bed. He fell on top of me, swearing up and down that he would never use a condom with me.

"Take it or leave it, the choice is yours," he said. "And just so you know, I do be using condoms when I go do my thing. With Shay, the condom came off. That's why I'm not sure about the baby."

"I don't believe you, but as long as you're out doin' your so-called *thing*, I hope you're good with me doin' my thing too. I just want to be sure, because it's not fair for you to do you, yet you got a problem with me doin' me."

Honey washed the smirk off his face and got serious. "You are doing you by being with me and only me. I don't want you with no one else, Karrine, and I mean that shit. You ain't got to get down like I do, and the truth is, I don't get down with as many bitches as I used to. I'm not saying that I've stopped cold turkey, but it ain't nothing like what it used to be. Give a nigga a little credit. I'm trying to be down with only you, and in due time I will."

See, this was my fault because I gave the okay for the open relationship bullshit. And even though the relationship was open, my legs remained closed to every nigga, with the exception of Honey. He had this shit under control, and I didn't like it one bit. I knew that things had to change because no nigga should ever be allowed to have this much control.

After Honey's dick finally settled down, he left to go to Maurice's party. I told him that I didn't want to go, but after sitting around at home doing nothing, I decided to put on some clothes and check out of here.

Before I left, I called Mama to check on Shania. Mama didn't answer the phone, so I left a message, telling her to call me back.

On my way to the club, I rocked some silver ankle leggings that looked painted on my light skin. My peep-toe metallic high heels sparkled with glitter, and the sleeveless jacket I wore was cut right underneath my breasts, revealing my bare midriff. I put on my new MAC lashes, and added shine to my short hair that had grown a bit and now swooped across my forehead. My sweet Nicki Minaj perfume was killing it, and so was I.

I couldn't wait to have some fun tonight, and I hadn't been to a club since Chyna, Simone, and me had gotten into trouble. I wanted to call them to see if they wanted to go out with me, but I knew that was a bad move. We'd all been staying out of trouble, and there was something about when we got together that gave us a need to show our asses. Our little meetings at Applebee's on Fridays were enough, and that was our opportunity to give each other the scoop about what had been going on in our lives.

From the outside, I could tell the club was already thick with a bunch of bitches and niggas. Since the line outside of the door was wrapped around the building, I parked my car in a lot where they charged twenty dollars. I tossed back a few swigs of Patrón and smoked some Kush before getting out of the car. Alcohol always helped me get my sexy on, and with a slightly blurred vision, I swished my hips from side to side, making my way to the door.

"Daaaang, that bitch fine," one nigga said as he nudged his friends, telling them to turn around. I just kept it moving, listening to the whistles, while another dude yelled for me to "come here."

Having a little clout, I saw one of Honey's boys working the front door. At first, he didn't recognize me, but when I mentioned Honey he snapped his finger.

"Yeah, I know who you are now. Come on. You can gon' ahead and go in there."

Hoes in line started hating. They were rolling their eyes and whispering about the bad bitch I was. Again, I didn't trip. What I learned from being in the club was that you had to keep your mouth clamped shut, or else you could find yourself getting fucked up by a gang of bitches that you didn't even know.

I stepped inside and was hit with loud hip-hop music that blasted throughout the joint. Spinning colorful lights hung from above, and there were plenty of partygoers getting it in on the hardwood dance floor. TVs were mounted on the wall, displaying images of certain people in the club so you could see who was there. It was muggy and hot as hell. After being there for five minutes, I started to sweat. I looked around for Honey, but already knew that he and his crew got down VIP style, so I looked around to find it.

As I sashayed through the crowd, I saw stairs that led to the upper level. Many people were up there looking down, and when I spotted Honey's barber, I figured he was somewhere up there. My heel touched the bottom stair, but a bouncer with a thick neck and deep voice stopped me.

"You can't go up there," he said with his arms folded, blocking me.

"I'm a guest for the party, and I was invited by Honey."

The bouncer looked me over, then moved aside to let me go up the burgundy-carpeted stairs. As my heels sunk into the plush carpet, I could hear much laughter and several dudes beefing about a basketball game. The music was just as loud upstairs, and the first person I saw was Honey. He was sitting at a square booth, surrounded by several bitches, while two niggas sat nearby. One light-bright bitch was twirling her fingers through his locs, and as my eyes shifted underneath the table, where I could see Honey's hand on her upper thigh. Everyone at the table was all smiles, and there were plenty of bottles of alcohol and Kush on the table.

From a distance, I watched. I watched Honey's hand creep slowly up the chick's thigh, but she crossed her legs so his hand couldn't go further. They smiled at each other, and when I saw her move closer to kiss him, I strutted forward.

Feeling as if I were moving in slow motion, I could barely hear the music. Everything was a blur, even when some disrespectful fool grabbed a chunk of my ass and squeezed it. I ignored him, because he was not a part of my mission. Honey was the only one in my sight, and all I could see was the royal blue, button-down shirt he rocked, and his blinding diamond and gold necklace that rested on his chest. I could see the black jeans he wore, as well as the leather belt he used to spank my ass with earlier. His locs looked fresh, and while some were tied back, most of them hung past his shoulders. His pearly whites were in full effect, until he looked up and locked his eyes with mine. After that, his smile vanished, and he eased his hand away from the chick who sat next to him.

Honey's friends followed the direction of his eyes, and they turned their heads to look at me. I saw one of the niggas reach behind his back, ready to pull something on me in case I tripped. Honey whispered something to him, and the nigga dropped his hands by his side. The chick next to him, as well as the others, glared at me from head to toe. When I reached the table, all of their eyes were glued to me.

"I need a seat," I said, looking directly at Honey. "It looks like the seats next to you are taken, so I guess you had better make room for me to sit on your lap."

Honey stood up and told the bitches next to him to move. They took their sweet little time, and every last ho at the table was rolling her eyes. Honey told everyone he would be right back, and he nudged his head for me to follow him. I surely didn't want to make a scene, but my blood was boiling.

"Looks like I've interrupted the party, huh?" I asked.

"You haven't interrupted nothing yet, but what's up? Why are you here?"

Shocked by his comment, I cocked my head back. "Nigga, I'm here because you invited me to come here."

"I invited you, but you declined. With that, I made some other arrangements."

"Really? Other arrangements like what? Are you sayin' that you invited someone else to come here with you?"

Honey licked his lips and sighed. "Yeah, I did. So check this out. You gon' need to make a move and check out of here. I'll be home no later than three, and if I go beyond that time, I'll do my best to call you."

I was straight-up in disbelief from what this nigga was saying. I knew he had been smoking that shit, but it normally didn't have him tripping like this. This couldn't have been the same Honey who had stood before me hours ago, telling me how much he loved me, licking my ass, and sharing how much I meant to him. Was this motherfucker serious? I actually laughed a little, thinking this nigga was joking. Honey, however, had a blank expression on his face, like he didn't see shit funny.

"Let me get this straight," I said. "You want me to leave, go back home, and wait for you to get there? I mean, like, where they do that shit at? Please tell me where?"

"I'm not doing this with you tonight, Karrine. If you got a problem with what I said, we'll talk about it when I get home. Just not right now."

He turned to walk away, but his ass didn't get too far. I could see everyone who was at the table watching us, and for him to turn away from me was hella embarrassing. I figured that if I put my hands on him he would probably fuck me up, so I had to think fast before I acted. I looked at the round, thick chocolate birthday cake sitting on a table next to me, so I picked it up. When I called Honey's name, he turned around and I tossed the cake at him, aiming it right at his face. Cake splattered everywhere. Mostly on his face, but much of it got on his clothes too.

"Daaaaamn," one dude shouted and laughed. "She fucked him up!"

Honey wiped down his face with his hand and reached for my arm, yanking it. "Bitch, is yo' ass crazy?" he yelled and pulled me toward the stairs. By then, his friendly bodyguards had shown up and they held me by my arms too.

"Let me go," I shouted and tussled to get away from them. But as I resisted, Honey grabbed my waist and tried to carry me over to the stairs. Everybody was looking at us, shaking their heads and laughing. Unable to get control of me like he wanted to, Honey slammed me on a nearby table.

"Hold her ass down," he said to the two goons who were helping him. They both held my arms while Honey popped the cap on a bottle of champagne and drenched my face with it.

"So, you wanna come in here and fuck up my whole night, huh? This here is for the cake, and there is more where that shit came from."

He opened another bottle and poured it all over my clothes and face again. I closed my eyes, hoping that shit wouldn't burn. I gagged as some of the champagne rushed into my nose, and I couldn't do shit, because those goons were still holding me down. The fat neck bouncer who had been at the end of the stairs came to help Honey.

"Get her the fuck out of here," Honey said. "And don't let her back in, because her ass is a troublemaker."

"You ain't seen trouble yet, nigga, just wait!"

The bouncer picked me up and tossed me over his shoulder. He carried me down the stairs, and I acted like a madwoman as I pounded the shit out of his back with my fists. All eyes were on me, and to say that shit was embarrassing would be an understatement.

When we reached the door, the bouncer threw me off of him. I landed on the hard concrete pavement. Honey had the nerve to stand there and watch. I was so damn mad at him that I rushed up from the ground and charged at him. The bouncer blocked me from getting to Honey, but when I took off my shoe and flung it at him, it didn't miss. It hit him right in the head, even though he tried to duck.

Being hit by the shoe caused Honey to come further outside and shove me.

"Take yo' ass home, ma, and quit trippin'. You up in here making a damn fool of yourself, and all you had to do was listen to me when I told you to go home."

I honestly could have gone to my car to get my gun and shot that nigga. I hated that he saw me near tears, so before I started to show my emotions I turned to walk away. With one shoe on and one shoe off, I limped down the street. Honey followed behind me, telling me to put on my shoe.

"You gon' cut yo' feet or get blisters on yo' damn feet," he said. "Take this shoe before I throw it."

I ignored Honey and kept on walking. By the time I reached my car and opened the door, he grabbed my waist and pushed the door shut. Since everybody was out of the nigga's sight, now he was singing a new tune.

"I didn't mean to hurt yo' feelings, but it ain't my fault that you said you weren't coming. Had I known you were, I never would've invited somebody else to come with me. Either way, I'll be home in an hour or so. Whatever you want to do or say to me, you can do it when I get there. Just not here, all right?"

I didn't say one word to Honey. He kissed my cheek and opened the car door for me. When I got inside, he closed the door. He started to walk toward the club, and I watched as he removed his cake stained shirt and wiped his face with it. A slow tear escaped from the corner of my eye, only because I hated how much I loved his ass. I could tell shit between us was spiraling out of control and we were on a downhill path. I felt so fucking stupid for allowing this shit to go on. This just wasn't me.

I was deep in thought, but I noticed two dudes walk by my car. One had his hands in his pockets, and the other looked at me from the corner of his eye. Both of them appeared real sneaky, and all kinds of vibes were going off. I quickly reached underneath my seat and rushed to open the car door. I could see the two niggas rushing up to get closer to Honey, who was not paying attention. He was several feet away from the club entrance, and as soon as I saw one of the dudes reach for a gun that was tucked in his pants, I aimed my Glock 9 at his head and fired. The first bullet whistled through the air and landed in back of the dude's neck. He dropped the gun and fell to his knees. He grabbed the wound, and couldn't even turn around to see where the bullet was fired from. The second bullet I fired missed the other dude, who had already broken out running. By then, though, Honey was coming my way, and he rushed up to me, yelling and screaming.

"Go get the muthafuckin' car!"

He reached for my Glock, but I didn't let him have it. I hurried to my car and he followed. He ordered me to get in on the passenger's side so he could drive. I barely closed the door before he sped off. The screeching tires burned rubber on the pavement, and several people were outside looking, trying to see what the hell was going on. Honey drove like a bat out of hell, trying to find the other nigga who had fled.

"Why were they tryin' to kill you?" I yelled.

Honey didn't answer my question. He cased several streets, but almost thirty minutes later, he gave up. He slammed his hand on the steering wheel and hurried back to the club. By then, the police were there, and gangs of people were crowded near the body on the ground that was covered by a white sheet. Instead of stopping, Honey just drove by and pulled his cell phone from his pocket. He called someone, but I didn't know who it was. The only thing he said was, "Meet me in about an hour. We got trouble."

After that, he ended the call and looked over at me. "Thanks for having my back," he said. "I owe you."

"I owe you, too." I reached over and slapped the shit out of him. "Nigga, I always got yo' back. But you damn sure better start havin' mine."

Honey wiggled his jaw and rubbed it. He didn't say shit else, but I could tell that motherfucker knew he had fucked up.

# HONEY

## 7

Hell, yes, I knew who the niggas were who tried to kill me. Right before Karrine had gotten to the club, I had a few words with those fools. One of the niggas hesitated to pay me the money he owed me. I'd given that fool almost a month to pay up, and if he thought he could take my product and not pay for it, he was sadly mistaken.

What most motherfuckers didn't understand was that when one man came up short, we were all short. When they failed to pay me, I had to pay out of my own pockets or risk the possibility of heat swinging my way. So this shit was real serious, as well as personal. More than anything, some niggas had to learn to treat this shit like a real business. For those who didn't, unfortunately, they had to be dealt with. Killing me would never solve their problems, and just because I had a slick mouth and was in control of things, that didn't mean shit. Niggas still had to pay up, and the thorough logs that I kept let my connections know who was handling their business the right way and who wasn't.

So as for today, I had one dead, stupid motherfucker who lost his life over a lousy five thousand dollars, and his friend, who just happened to be in the wrong place at the wrong time.

"I swear to God that I didn't have nothin' to do with Jamal's plan to shoot you. I didn't even know that nigga had a gun on him, that's why I ran."

My boys Juan and Maurice circled the young punk who was tied to a chair, unable to get loose. Sweat beads dotted his entire face, and the nigga had already pissed on himself because Juan made him suck on the tip of his Glock, as if it were a dick.

We were in the basement of a rental property I owned and used to handle this kind of business. Many niggas had lost their lives and taken their last breaths right here in the same chair this fool sat in.

I leaned against a table with my arms folded. My eyes were focused on the teary-eyed nigga who begged me to spare his life.

"If yo' ass was so innocent," I said. "Then why did you run? Had it been me, I would have hung around to defend myself."

"Me too," Juan said. "'Cause when you run, that means yo' ass guilty of somethin'.'"

Juan pushed the swinging light bulb that hung over the nigga's head. It was the only source of light that shined in the dim, concrete basement. Water from a leaking faucet dripped, and as everything fell silent, the water was all any of us could hear.

"I . . . the only reason I ran was because I was scared. You gotta believe me, Honey, and I ain't have no reason whatsoever to want to do you like that. That beef we had earlier was squashed. I figured that nigga Jamal was gon' get you ya money and we'd be done with it."

I tilted my head from left to right, trying to ease the tension in my neck. When the phone rang, I hit the intercom button, knowing exactly who it was, because I had been waiting on her to call.

"Speak," I said, letting her know I was on the other end.

"I will," Mama said. "But tell me who all is in the room."

"Me, Maurice, Juan, and the stupid muthafucka I told you about. He says he didn't have shit to do with the attempt on my life, and even if I do believe him, I'm still short five grand."

"According to your monthly total, you're down about thirty grand. You need to get those niggas to pay up. I don't like it that money has to keep coming out of our pockets and the losses are starting to sting."

"I feel you on that, and I'm sending some of my collectors out today to minimize the financial damage. I'll let you know how that goes, but my question to you is what do you want me to do with this nigga I got here? You know I don't get down with shit like this, unless I get the word from you."

Mama paused for a few seconds before saying anything. "You always want to hurt somebody and you need to stop that shit, Honey. Can that nigga hear me?"

I looked at the frightened dude who nodded his head. "Yeah, he can hear you. Loud and clear."

"What's your name?" Mama asked.

"Quincy Bailey," he said.

"Quincy, you really didn't try to kill my Honey, did you?"

"No . . . no ma'am, I didn't. That shit wasn't on me, I swear."

"That's good to know, because can you imagine how devastated I would've been, if somebody had to call and tell me my son had been killed?"

"I . . . I can't even imagine it, and I know it would've been hard for you to swallow."

"Right. Real hard, and no mother should have to go through that. Do you have a decent relationship with your mother?"

"Yep, yes, ma'am, we good, and it would break her heart if anything ever happened to me."

"I'm sure it would, but we all got to go sooner or later. I wouldn't want to put her in a situation like that, because our kids are real special to us, if you know what I mean."

"I do," ole boy rushed to say. "I know exactly what you mean."

"That's good. Now, how many kids do you have, Q? I can call you Q, can't I?"

"Yes, ma'am, and I have about three . . . no, four of them. I just had a son about two months ago."

"Awww, congrats. You say you got four kids—what are their names?"

"Uh, Q Junior, Vonzell . . ." he paused and looked up at the ceiling. "Portia and, uh, Wesley."

"Damn, you got four kids and it took you that long to name them? Sounds like you're a deadbeat daddy, Q, are you?"

"No, I wouldn't say all of that. I will say that I do what I can, when I can do it."

Mama laughed. "Yeah, you sound like a deadbeat. And you know what, Quincy? I don't like deadbeat niggas. I think they take up too much space and they fuck up too many lives. If I was there, I would blow yo' goddamn brains out myself. But since I'm not, Juan or Honey will have the pleasure of doing it. Honey, rock-a-bye that piece-of-shit-ass nigga. I gotta go see about my grandbaby, so I'll call you later."

Mama ended the call, and I looked at Juan. He raised his gun and placed it on the side of the scary nigga's temple.

"Please," he begged with tears streaming down his face and turning his head to look at Juan. "Don't do it."

"I'm not," Juan said, looking at Maurice. The code was, if Mama didn't mention your name, then the deed was yours to do. With pleasure, while Quincy had his head turned, begging Juan not to do it, Maurice put two bullets in the back of his head. Blood splattered, and the chair crashed to the concrete floor with the dead nigga in it.

I shrugged and looked at Juan. "I thought Mama liked him. That nigga should've kept his mouth shut about them kids, and didn't he know where she was going with that shit?"

We all laughed, and I let Juan and Maurice clean up. I made my way upstairs, and when I checked my cell phone, Karrine had called twice, but she didn't leave a message. I was about to hit her back, but I'd gotten a text message from Kita, the chick I was at the club with, asking if I was still coming over. Since we didn't get a chance to get our fuck on after the party, I told her earlier I would stop by. But the truth was, I wasn't feeling up to that shit. I kind of felt bad about how things went down with me and Karrine. I seriously wasn't trying to diss her, but she was the one who said she didn't want to go to the party with me. It wasn't my fault that she didn't want to go, and just because she had changed plans, it didn't mean that I had to. My plans were locked in, and Karrine had to learn how to play by my rules, not hers.

While I loved so much about her, the problem was that she had become boring as hell. All we did was fuck all the time, and a nigga needed a little bit more excitement in his life. Since Shania had been born, Karrine had changed. I understood that she was trying to do the motherly thing, but it didn't mean that she had to stop living.

Every time I suggested that we do something together, she made excuses. I didn't appreciate that shit, so I kept on doing me, and was doing me quite well. I was, however, glad that she had shown her ass up that night. And I would for damn sure take cake in my face instead of a bullet in my back. I had to do something real sweet for her saving my life, but for now I had to go see what was up with Kita. She had just sent me a naked photo of her playing with her fat pussy, and it was looking real sweet to me. If anything, I'd rather be dipping into that shit, instead of going home and listening to Karrine gripe about bullshit that she couldn't do nothing about. A nigga needed a little relaxation sometimes, so it was possible that I wouldn't see Karrine until tomorrow.

# KARRINE

# 8

I hadn't said much to Honey about what had happened the other night, and he was waiting on me to get my clown on when he came through the door on Saturday morning, right before seven.

The first thing he did was take a shower, and then he had the nerve to turn to me, asking where his breakfast was. I wanted to tell him to go back to that bitch who had him smelling like hot pussy. But I kept my mouth shut. He already knew I was headed to Cali to get Shania, and all he said when I left was that he'd see me when I got back. After that, he laid on the couch and took his ass to sleep.

I jetted, and several hours later, I was at Mama's house, holding my pretty girl in my arms. Mama was in the kitchen frying some chicken, and her friend, Trice, sat across from me at the table polishing her nails. Mama was trying to talk me into letting Shania stay, but I wasn't down with it.

"She's been over here for almost two weeks straight, Mama. If I let her keep stayin' here like this, she gon' think you her Mama, instead of me."

"And what's wrong with that? Trice, do you see anything wrong with that?"

"No, I don't. Besides, you're a good mother."

"Damn good mother," Mama added.

"I didn't say you weren't," I said. "What I'm sayin' is, you already have your three, lovely daughters. Allow me to have mine."

Mama rolled her eyes and placed several pieces of chicken on her plate. She brought the plate over to the table and reached for Shania, who had her arms out to her.

"That's a shame," I said, handing Shania over to Mama. "Go ahead and enjoy these last few hours with her," I teased. "We ain't comin' back for one whole month."

"Girl, if you pull that shit on me, I will come to Chicago and raise hell. But I know I don't have to worry about that, because Honey will bring my baby to me anytime I want to see her."

"Yeah, and Honey will fuck around and get his feelings hurt, too. Seriously."

Trice laughed, showing her stained teeth. She had been Mama's friend for many years, and Mama trusted her a lot. Not more than she trusted Honey, though.

"Sounds like trouble in paradise. Is there?" Trice asked.

I started to tell Mama and Trice about all the mess Honey had been doing. Both of them shook their heads, and Mama looked pissed. She kept rolling her eyes and releasing deep breaths.

"Yep, that sounds like Honey," Trice said. "But the two of you make a great couple. Y'all will work it out."

"Don't feed her that bullshit, Trice," Mama said. "Honey is a dog-ass muthafucka who Karrine needs to get the fuck away from. I told you before that nigga wasn't no good, but you keep on chasing after that dick, so you deserve everything you got coming. I know that's not what you want to hear, Karrine, but I'm just keeping it real with you."

"This ain't about no dick, Mama. The reason that I stay with Honey is strictly out of love."

Mama threw her hand back at me. "Girl, tell that bull-shit to somebody else. I've seen his dick and I witnessed with my own eyes what that shit can do to a woman's pussy. If he makes you have more than two orgasms during a thirty minute sex session, you fucked."

Mama and Trice laughed and high-fived each other. I didn't see much of anything funny.

"Whatever, Mama. You say it's a dick thing, but I say it's a love thing. I may be losin' control over what's been goin' on in our relationship, and if you want to offer me some advice, tell me what I need to do to get him to start seein' things my way and to stop believin' the grass is greener on the other side."

"That nigga don't care if the grass on the other side is green, blue, purple or pink. He still gon' stick his dick into it, and that is something that you will have to face. You won't be able to tame Honey, because that nigga loves pussy, and one little ole tight pussy won't do. Either you can accept that shit or move on. Second, stop playing by his rules and get yo' ass out of the house. Have some fun. Air your pussy out and free it from one damn dick. What I know about Honey is this. He don't want no weak bitch sitting at home all day, griping, crying, and waiting on him to come home and fuck her. He wants a woman who will challenge him. You know . . . do shit that will surprise the fuck out of him and stop being so basic. Right now, he knows you're down with him, no matter what. Sometimes, niggas tend to take advantage of that shit, but wake his ass up. I surely thought I had taught you better that this, Karrine, and you had better get with the program before it's too late. If not, you gon' find yourself hating the very nigga you say you love and pumping bullets into his head. Whatever you do, don't let history repeat itself. I hope you remember what happened between me and Ray."

I heard Mama loud and clear. Everything she had said was so right. I had to do something different, because the way I was handling things right now wasn't working out.

Since Mama wanted me to "find myself," she suggested that I chill with her for the week. After that, she talked me into letting Shania stay with her until I worked out my issues with Honey. Throughout the week, Honey had been calling, trying to find out when I would be coming home. It sounded as if he'd been missing me, and by Friday, he surprised me when he showed up at Mama's house.

We were chilling by the poolside, and Mama got in his shit about what I had told her. His face was twisted from listening to her harsh words, and he couldn't stop staring at me with an evil eye.

"This is why I didn't want the two of y'all involved with each other," Mama griped. "Y'all gon' get me caught in the middle of this shit, and I'ma have to put my foot in somebody's ass. Probably yours, Honey, because if you don't want to do her right then don't go setting up house. Free Karrine and let her go about her own damn business."

"No can do," Honey said, placing his hands behind his head while relaxing on the lounging chair. I sat between his legs with my yellow bikini on. Trice and Shania were in the pool, and I kept watching them while tuned into the conversation between Mama and Honey.

"You're asking me to free somebody who I love, and I'm not going to do that," Honey said. "Besides, Karrine already knows what's up. We good for each other, and she knows that just as much as I do."

I turned my head to look at him. "No, I really don't know what's up. And if or whenever I want you to free me, you will."

I stood up and pulled my bikini bottoms out of my ass that had swallowed it. I went inside to use the bathroom, and as soon as I came out, Honey was waiting for me.

"Why you tell yo' crazy-ass Mama about our relationship? You know she gon' be getting in yo' head and talking that dumb shit. The last thing we need right now is for her to be involved in our personal lives."

I folded my arms and looked up at him. "I can talk to Mama about anything that I wish to. If you don't like it, then stop actin' like a stupid-ass nigga and man yo' ass up."

I tried to walk away, but Honey pushed me into the bathroom and shut the door. He turned out the lights, putting us into pure darkness. I felt his hands touch my bikini bottoms, and when he attempted to pull them down, I put my hand over his to stop him.

"Tell me this," he said, moving closer to me. "Is it really that bad being with me? Am I truly making yo' life that miserable?"

"Yes," I said being honest. "I don't like where you're taking us, Honey, and you've been so disrespectful to me that I can't stand it."

"If I say I'm sorry, you won't believe me. What I'll do is agree with you and see what I can do to make shit better."

Honey lowered my bikini bottoms to the floor and removed his swim trunks. He hiked my legs up around his waist and I straddled the front of him. I could feel his hardness resting between my slit, and after he maneuvered himself in the right position, he entered me. There I was again, under his spell and enjoying every stroke that he was giving me. Mama was so right about those orgasms, and within thirty minutes, I was already on number three. Honey held me against the door, knocking my fucking back out. The feel of his big dick turning circles in me made me holler. I hollered so loudly that when there was a knock at the door, Honey had to place his hand over my mouth.

"Who is it?" he asked.

"Who in the fuck do you think it is?" Mama said. "And I know one thing. When this bathroom door opens, I betta not smell sex. Y'all need to do that shit on y'all time, not mine and definitely not in my house!"

Honey paid Mama no mind. He started pumping faster, trying to make me cum again, and he wanted to bust a nut. Since there was nothing but silence, Mama hit the door again.

"What?" Honey shouted.

"Open this goddamn door. Now!"

"Give me a minute," he said. "Ju . . . just one more minute."

I wanted to bust out laughing. That was until I felt a loud pound on the door.

"Is she kickin' it," I whispered to Honey.

He didn't respond. A few seconds later, the door sounded as if it cracked when Mama hit or kicked it again. I pushed Honey's shoulder back and whispered for him to back away from me. "We can finish up later. She trippin' too hard for me."

Honey pulled out of me and hurried to put on his swimming trunks. I barely got my bikini bottoms on before he opened the door to face Mama. She turned on the light and sniffed the air.

"Get y'all trifling-asses out of my fucking house. Right now!"

At first, me and Honey thought Mama was playing, but she was serious as hell. She straight-up sent us packing and told us not to come back until we learned how to show her some respect.

Honey and I sat at the airport in disbelief, waiting for our plane to depart. When it did, we became members of the Mile High Club and got our fuck on, on the plane. By the time we got home, I was exhausted and so was Honey. I fell asleep in his arms, but was awakened by the numerous phone calls that he'd gotten. One call he stepped away to take. I could tell it was a bitch because of the sly smirk on his face. No doubt, this shit was working me.

The next day, I met Chyna at her job. She called to tell me that she had hooked up an interview for me with her boss, but when I got there, I was surprised to find out that her boss was more than a boss. He was her new man, and she couldn't wait to introduce him to me.

"Desmon, this is my sister, Karrine," Chyna said as we went into his office. "My hope is that you'll be able to find her a position within the company."

Desmon stood up to shake my hand. Chyna had done real good, and quite frankly, so had Simone. She was still dating one of her professors, and Desmon came off as an educated businessman who had his shit together. He was fine as ever, and the tailored suit he wore clung to his athletic frame perfectly. I was impressed, and I hoped that my constant stares didn't make him or Chyna uncomfortable.

"Have a seat," he said. "I want to hear all about your experience—tell me why I should hire you for the customer service position?"

Chyna excused herself from the room, leaving us alone. Unfortunately, the only customer service experience I had to offer him was what I had learned through video porn, but I couldn't tell him about that. Since Honey had been providing for me, technically, I didn't have shit to talk to Desmon about. What I did, though, was share the experience I had from doing volunteer work several years ago, and I'd also done some work for a non-profit organization. I couldn't tell if Desmon was satisfied with my answers or not. All he did was jot down things on a piece of paper and nod his head.

He reminded me so much of Idris Elba and seemed much older than Chyna. But as far as I saw it, she had hit the jackpot. I thought that way for a while, but then I got a glimpse of his ring. My eyes scanned his office, and that was when I noticed him in several pictures with another woman I assumed to be his wife.

After twenty more minutes, the interview was over. Desmon told me that he would be in touch, and then he thanked me for coming. I thanked him too. Chyna was waiting for me in the lobby. She looked real nice in her navy blue suit and white shirt. I had never seen her look so classy, and she had a real glow about her.

"So, how did it go?" she asked as we walked to the elevator together.

"It went okay. I didn't have much experience to share with him, and I started to tell his ass how much cash I made doin' video porn."

Chyna laughed. "It wouldn't have surprised him because I already told him what was up with that. No matter what, I do believe the job is yours if you want it. Did he say when he was goin' to call you?"

"He didn't say. Just said he would be in touch. But on another note, I saw the ring on his finger. He's fine as fuck, but please tell me that nigga ain't married."

The elevator opened, and Chyna held the door open for me. "I'll call you later to tell you all about that little problem."

"Uh, please do, because you know we don't get down like that, right?"

"Yeah, well, speak for yourself. I have my reasons."

I gave Chyna a quick hug and got on the elevator. I started thinking about her situation, as well as Simone's. It seemed as if they'd made some real progress in their lives. But there I was, still playing the shoot-'em-up games and dealing with Honey's bullshit. I hoped that Desmon called me. That would be the first step to reviving my life.

After I left Chyna's job, I didn't want to go back home, so I headed to the gym. I hadn't spoken to Simone in a few days, and since we missed our Applebee's outing, I asked her to meet me at the gym so we could workout together. She said she would, and by the time I had gotten there, Simone beat me there.

"Ugh, you make me so sick," I said after seeing how spectacular she looked in her spandex.

"Please," she smiled then gave me a hug. "Look at you. I can't even tell you had a baby, and look at you in those itty-bitty shorts. All I can say is, don't bend over in here, okay?"

"I'll try not to." I stepped on the elliptical machine next to the one Simone was on. "And as far as this figure goes, you can't see the bulge in my belly right now. It's there, and I really need to work it off."

"Well, do what you gotta do. Either way, you still look good."

It was good to hear those compliments. Not only from Simone, but we managed to turn a lot of heads as we worked out. We talked about everything from the professor to Honey. From school to Mama. When video porn became the subject, I couldn't believe that Simone said she still indulged herself, especially after all that had happened.

"Girl, that shit was easy money," she said. "I'm just real careful this time around, and I play strictly by the book. No meetings, no more than thirty minutes at a time, and no late payments. Don't be mad at me for still doin' it, but I just can't seem to work for less than fifteen dollars an hour. It's hard out here, and a sista gotta do what she must do to get paid. I respect what Chyna is doin', but she also got that rich motherfucker waitin' on her hand and foot. You got Honey makin' it rain money for you, so y'all all good."

"I wouldn't say all that, and I'm not mad at you at all. Do you and do you well. I may have to make a move in that direction again, so please know that I'm not judgin' you."

"Girl, please. Honey will kill yo' ass if he ever saw you doin' that shit again. He already told you he didn't want you to do that, didn't he?"

"Well, what Honey wants he don't always get. I—"

I turned my head when this brotha came up to us, interrupting our conversation. "I was getting ready to check out of here," he said to me. "But something wouldn't let me leave without coming over here to say what's up to you. I also wondered if I could get your phone number and holla at you later."

Had he been an ugly motherfucker, I would have kept it moving on the elliptical machine. Since he was sexy and fine as hell, had that dark chocolate, smooth skin like Honey, and his hair was flowing with deep waves, my exercising came to a halt. I searched into his light brown eyes and was almost hooked.

"Before I give you my number, wouldn't you like to know my name?" I asked.

"Right," Simone said. "Especially since you've gotten to know her ass already."

I guess she noticed that he was looking at my ass, too.

Taking no offense to what Simone said, he smiled and cleared his throat. "Your name would be nice, and just so you know, my name is Eric."

"Eric, I'm Karrine. Nice to meet you. When I toss out these digits to you, you'll have to keep them in your head."

"I don't have my phone to log the numbers in, so I guess I have to keep them in my head. Go ahead and give them to me."

I called off my phone number to Eric. After hollering at me and Simone for a few more minutes, he left. I turned to Simone and shrugged my shoulders.

"Cute," I said, sizing him up. "Very sexy, but not as tall and fine as my Honey."

Simone rolled her eyes. "Well, every nigga can't look like Honey, but Eric wasn't bad lookin' at all. You need to see what's up with that, and do you see what happens when you finally get out of the crib and start livin' a little?"

"Yeah, I do, but I swear you are startin' to sound more and more like Chyna and Mama every day. That wouldn't be because you bitches been talkin' about me, would it?"

Simone laughed. "Only just a little bit, but you know we all want what's in yo' best interest, so it's all good."

I was sure it was, so I didn't trip. We finished exercising and parted ways. On the way to my car, my cell phone rang. I didn't recognize the number, but I answered anyway.

"Karrine?" the person said.

"Yes."

"This is Eric. Just wanted to make sure you didn't play me and give me the wrong number."

I laughed. "Now, why would I do that? If I didn't want you to have my number, I wouldn't have given it to you."

"That's good to know, but all women don't think like you do. I'm just glad we can hook up, and now that I know we can, tell me what you got going on this evening."

"I must say that you really don't waste much time, do you?"

"No, I don't. My parents always taught me that whenever you wanted something to go after it. If not, you'll let a good thing pass you by. So how about dinner tonight? Seven o'clock at your favorite restaurant."

"How about I think on this and call you back in an hour or so to let you know?"

"I can deal with that. Get at me when you can, hopefully soon."

I ended the call, not sure what I would be getting myself into. I wasn't even sure if I would be wasting my time, especially since my feelings for Honey were so damn strong.

When I got home, as usual, he wasn't there. I checked my messages and he did leave a message, telling me to call him. When I did, I'll be damned if a bitch didn't answer his phone. I thought I'd had the wrong number until I heard Honey cussing her ass out. He then got on the phone.

"Who this?" he asked.

I hung up. He called right back, but I refused to answer. Almost an hour later, he came home, but by then, I had already called Eric and told him that I would meet him at Olive Garden tonight.

I didn't have time to play these ongoing games with Honey, and it surprised him when he came through the door and saw me chilling back while eating ice cream and watching TV in the family room.

"Was that you who called me?" he asked then sat next to me on the couch.

"Yep, it was me, but since somebody else answered your phone, I figured you were busy."

"I was with Shay, talking to her about the baby situation. She admitted that the baby wasn't mine. I'm real damn happy about that shit, for real."

All I did was nod and continued to show disinterest. Deep down it was good news, because I didn't want another bitch to have his baby.

Honey took my spoon from my hand and scooped up some of my ice cream, eating it. "What's for dinner?" he asked. "Do you want to go somewhere to eat, or do you want to come with me tonight and watch me play the tables? We hooked up a private room at the casino, and if you want to come you can."

"Naw, I'ma pass on that. I'm hangin' out with Chyna and some of her friends tonight. She invited me to a birthday party, so I'ma see what's up with that."

Honey stood up and stretched. He went upstairs, and thirty minutes later, he came back dressed to impress in a pair of black slacks and a gray V-neck shirt that showed many of the tattoos on his arms. Some of his locs were tied back, and he had trimmed the hair that suited his chin into a goatee. His cologne infused the air, and I seriously started to change my plans for tonight and go with him.

"I'll be home late," he said. "Have your phone available so I can reach you."

"Have yours available too, but this time, see if you can answer it instead of somebody else."

Honey ignored my comment. He leaned in to give me a kiss then left.

I waited until I saw him pull out of the driveway before I went upstairs to get ready for my date with Eric. After my shower, I put on a mustard color stretch dress that cut above my knees. Adding gold to my fit, I wrapped a thick belt around my waist and slid into my strappy gold, five-inch heels.

The softness of the stretch dress felt good against my skin and it fit my curves perfectly. Without a bra or panties on, I felt sexy as ever. I added sweetness to me with Nicki's perfume, and I left around six fifteen so I wouldn't be late.

I arrived at Olive Garden early, but ten minutes later, Eric came through the door. He looked even better than he did earlier. This time he wore jeans, a jacket, and a T-shirt underneath. I could tell he was older than I was, probably older than Honey too.

Eric looked me over and smiled. He reached for my hand and put it on his chest.

"You feel that," he said.

I laughed. "What? Your rapid heartbeat?"

"Yeah, but do you feel how fast it's beating? It sped up when I saw you, and all I gotta say is damn you look good."

I blushed and thanked Eric for the compliment. I told him how nice he looked too, and then we followed the hostess, who seated us at a table.

Minutes later, a waiter came to take the order for our drinks. Keeping it simple, I ordered a diet Coke, and Eric got lemonade. We were ready to indulge ourselves in a heavy conversation, to get to know each other, but when I looked up and saw Honey coming my way, my eyes grew wide.

Honey had a blank expression on his face. He approached the table, and without saying anything he pulled back a chair and sat in it.

"I don't mean to interrupt, but somebody forgot to invite me to dinner. Has the waiter been over here yet?" he asked.

I was so stunned that I couldn't say shit. Eric hadn't said anything either. Honey, however, flagged down the waiter.

"I'll need another menu, and you can get me a glass of ice water? I don't see the breadsticks and salad either, so when you get time can you bring those too?" The waiter nodded. He started to walk away, but Honey grabbed his arm. "Wine," he said. "We need some wine to celebrate. Bring us a bottle of the best thing you got."

"Will do," the waiter said with a forced smile. He could tell something wasn't right, and so could a few other people who sat nearby.

Honey rubbed his hands then clinched them together on the table. "So," he said, looking at Eric. "How long have you been fucking Karrine?"

Eric looked over at me and shrugged his shoulders. I hurried to speak up. "It ain't even like that. He's just a friend and I met him here for dinner. Besides, I thought you were goin' to the casino?"

"I asked this nigga a question, not you. But since you opened your big ass mouth, I thought you were going out with Chyna? I guess that shit fell through, especially since Chyna just happens to be on her way to California to chill with yo' Mama. The next time you want to include her in yo' lies, you'd better check with her first."

The waiter brought over three wine glasses, a bottle of wine and breadsticks. "The salad will be here shortly. May I pour the wine for you?"

Honey took the bottle from the waiter's hand. "Naw, I got this. Thanks, now move on."

The waiter forced another smile then walked away. Honey poured out three glasses of wine and lifted his glass. "Help yourselves, and drink up," he said to me and Eric. "I don't know what y'all want to drink to, but I'ma drink to yo' lying ass, Karrine. May you take another minute or two to enjoy the breadsticks. After that, you got two minutes to get yo' ass up from this table, or else I'ma knock the shit out of you for thinking it's okay for you to have dinner with this nerdy-ass nigga. Going beyond that two minutes gon' get a lot of people hurt, so think fast. The next few minutes are in your control."

Honey tossed back the wine and reached for one of the breadsticks. He put it in his mouth and looked at his watch. I swallowed the lump in my throat and looked across the table at Eric, who I didn't want to get involved in this shit. He remained calm.

"Maybe we can do this some other time," he said. "Just call me later."

"Smart man," Honey said, turning to him. "But just so you know, there won't be no later, right Karrine?"

Right then, the manager came over to the table, asking if everything was okay.

"Perfectly fine," Honey said, standing up. "My bitch was just getting ready to wash her hands of this nigga, and if you would like to stay here and witness it, you can."

"Bitch?" I said with a scrunched face. "Really?"

"Don't act all brand new, ho, you heard me. Now get the fuck up and let's go. You've wasted enough of my time with this bullshit."

I opened my mouth, but before I could say anything, Honey snatched me up from the table so quickly that the wine spilled on my dress. By now, everyone was looking and the manager asked us to leave. Eric stood up when Honey shoved me toward the door. I stumbled in my high heels and Honey walked up to Eric, standing face to face with him.

"You really shouldn't be treating her like that," he said to Honey. "That shit is real disrespectful."

"So muthafuckin' what, nigga? What yo' punk-ass gon' do about it?"

Eric mean mugged Honey, who towered over him by a few inches.

"Yeah, that's what I thought. Nothing. Now pay the goddamn bill and shut the fuck up. Don't call Karrine again, and if you do, I'ma break every last one of your fingers off and shove them up yo' ass."

Honey walked away. He snatched my hand and pulled me out of the front door with him.

"Would you stop all of this?" I said, barely able to keep my balance because of his abrupt pace. He let go of my hand and walked up to his SUV.

"Get in the damn truck," he ordered.

I halted my steps and didn't move. Honey narrowed his eyes and sucked his teeth. "Karrine, don't make me hurt you. I said get in the truck. Don't make me say that shit again."

So many people were already looking, and I didn't want to embarrass myself anymore. Plus, I had a feeling that the police would be coming soon, so the quicker we got away from this scene the better.

I got into Honey's truck with him and he sped off the parking lot. For whatever reason, he seemed calmer. "So, what's up with you and that nigga? And don't lie to me, Karrine, because I've been following yo' ass."

"If you've been followin' me then you know that ain't nothin' up with us. I just met him today, and I accepted his dinner offer."

"Yeah, and you were about to accept his offer for something else, too. It's bad enough you running out to dinner and lying to me about that shit, but why you ain't got no bra or panties on? Yo' ass was thinking about fucking that nigga, weren't you?"

I didn't say a word, because I didn't want to get caught in another lie. I probably would've given up the goodies tonight, only because I was ready to try something different.

"Answer my question, Karrine. Was you gon' fuck that nigga or not?"

"I don't want to say, because I don't know what would've happened. And why are you so worried about me, when you out here fuckin' whoever the hell you want to. I'm not feeling how this shit is goin' down, and what's good for you will be good for me too."

Honey pulled over to the curb and slammed on the brakes. He got out of his truck and walked over to passenger's side. After he pulled the door open, he unzipped his pants but left them hanging off his ass. He pulled his hard dick out then turned me around to face him. While touching my hips, he tried lifting my dress up.

"I'll show you what's good for you. And it's the only thing that's good for you, nothing or no one else is."

"No," I said, pushing his chest back and trying to keep my legs shut. "This is not the only damn thing good for me. Do you really think your dick got what it takes to solve all of our problems?"

Honey struggled to pry my legs apart, and when I could no longer hold off his pressure, my legs opened. He lifted my dress over my ass and held my hips. He scooted me in closer to him and forced his dick inside of me.

"I didn't know we had any problems, and since you don't open yo' mouth to tell me about them, how am I supposed to know that you're not happy with the way things are? You gotta open yo' mouth and tell me what's up, ma. Stop leaving me to assume shit, because I be assuming that shit is all good with us. Not perfect, but good enough. Lastly, the only reason I called you those names at the restaurant was because I wanted to upset that nigga. I wanted to know if he would put me in my place for disrespecting you, but you saw that weak nigga didn't do shit, didn't you? You don't want no punk-ass fool like that, do you? You know I would never let a muthafucka talk to you like that, and if he said that shit to you around me, that nigga would be dead right now."

I wasn't sure what Honey was trying to prove, but he leaned in further, causing me to fall back on my elbows. He rocked my pussy well and had me wrapping my legs around his back, enjoying the ride. Maybe I hadn't told him how I was really feeling about our relationship. The reason why was because I figured it wouldn't matter. I doubted that Honey would change who he was, and the only question that needed to be answered was if I would deal with his ways. Right now, I was dealing with it. I was dealing with his satisfying dick that was tearing my insides up. I threw my arms around his neck and pulled on his locs as our bodies rocked together. Several cars drove by—some slowing down to take a peek, others blowing their horns at us. We didn't care who was watching, and this moment was all about us.

"Promise me that you won't ever call that nigga again. Your word is bond, Karrine, so don't say it unless you mean it."

I didn't hesitate. "Why do I need him when I got you? All of you, and that's already more than I can handle."

"You damn right it is."

Honey and I finished up. Afterward, we went to the casino where I watched him blow twenty-five thousand dollars within an hour. Several hours after that he was only down by ten, and by the time the night was over, he was up by seven.

As I sat on his lap, I dabbed the sweat from his forehead with a napkin. "Whew. I was almost worried for a minute there. Glad you made a comeback," I said.

"I always do," he boasted. "And that's what happens when you stick with a real winner. Remember that."

Honey winked and got back to his game.


Over the next few weeks, things were going okay. Shania had been home for two weeks, then she was right back with Mama. Honey and I had been coping, and we were always on our best behavior when Shania was at home. We also had a long talk, and I laid everything on the line for him. He could no longer say he didn't know how I felt, because I had told him.

I told him how I wanted . . . needed some things to change. All he'd said was that over time things would get better, and that I had to understand his priority was business. Somewhere after the business thing, I and Shania fell in. But the truth was, I wasn't happy about that. I knew he was in deep with Mama, but a huge part of me wanted Honey to let that shit go. His life was always at risk, and he had definitely been living on the edge. He was still coming and going as he pleased, and when I faced reality, Honey was still being Honey. So for now, I was content. Content, but not complacent because I had been talking to Eric. While Honey was gone, Eric and I spent hours and hours on the phone talking. I'd gotten to know more about him and I liked his style. I liked how he made me laugh, and I appreciated his compliments. I apologized to him about what had happened during dinner, and while Honey was in Cali with Mama and Shania, Eric invited me to his place.

At first, I was reluctant to go. Then I'd thought about the hold Honey still had on me and decided what the hell? Honey had already made me turn down the customer service position Desmon had offered to me, and Honey's reason was that it didn't make sense for me to work a nine-to-five job when I had access to all the money I needed. Chyna was so mad at me for not accepting the position. She said I had wasted her time, so she wasn't speaking to me. I understood that she was upset, but her worries should have been on that married man she was fucking with, not me.

I dolled myself up in tight jeans, heels, and a sleeveless, silk shirt that plumped up my breasts and made them appear rounder. Before going to Eric's house, I called Honey just to be 100 percent sure that he was still in Cali. He said he was, but when I asked to speak to Mama, he told me that her, Trice, and Shania were at the grocery store. Once we ended our call, I called

Mama just to be sure. Her voice mail came on. I left her a message, telling her to call me back soon then I went to Eric's crib.

Eric's loft was laid the fuck out. The moment he opened the door, my eyes started to wander. The open space was humongous and the whole place was decked out with contemporary furniture.

Over the past several weeks we had gotten comfortable with each other. He told me that he worked from home and had an online booming business where he sold certain products to make a profit. On the tour through his loft, he showed me his office that was in a closed-off room, and the other spacious room he showed me was his bedroom. It was surrounded by large windows that overlooked downtown Chicago. Everything was real tidy and clean, and I was impressed by how well Eric seemed to have it going on.

"Can I get you anything to drink?" he asked as I sat on the cream colored leather sofa.

"I could use somethin' a little strong," I said. "If you got it."

"Coming right up."

Eric whipped up two drinks in the kitchen then brought them over to the table. He gave me my drink, and after one sip, I gagged.

"Wha . . . what in the hell did you put in there?" I asked.

"A mixture of everything," Eric admitted. "You told me to make it strong, so I did."

"No doubt about that." I laughed then took another sip.

Within the hour, Eric and I both were fucked up. We found ourselves ripping each other's clothes off and grinding against each other, right outside of the door that led to his bedroom. I reached down to grab his package, just to make sure it was suitable. It was. I appreciated the length, as well as the thickness of it.

"Let's go into the bedroom," Eric suggested in a whisper, between our sloppy kisses. I followed him to his bedroom, and as I dropped back on his bed with no clothes on and opened my legs, he put a condom on and got on top of me. He positioned my legs over his shoulders, but as he broke into my pussy, a flash of Honey appeared before me. I couldn't stop thinking about him. After all of Eric's hard efforts to make me cum, I just couldn't go there. Somewhere within the hour, my pussy had dried up and Eric's deep thrusts began to feel painful.

I wasn't sure if he had noticed how dry I was or not, but when he pulled out of me and started to suck my pussy, that was when I finally released an orgasm. It wasn't much to brag about. I added a little something extra to it, just so he wouldn't feel as though I wasn't pleased.

"Your pussy tastes so sweet and good," he said, licking across his wet lips. "How I wish that you were mine. You gon' be mine, aren't you?"

I damn sure didn't want to lie, but as of right now, I refused to answer his question. I was confused. I felt guilty for being there, and why was I feeling as if this was so wrong? I wasn't sure, but I stayed with Eric until three o'clock in the morning. When I got up to put on my clothes, he rolled over in bed.

"You're leaving already?" he asked.

"Yeah, my daughter will be home later, and I want to get some rest before she comes. I had a nice time, though. Thanks for invitin' me to come over."

Eric pulled the covers aside and got out of bed. "I hope you'll be coming again. And know that the door is always open."

Eric put on his jeans and walked me outside to my car. We kissed and I told him I'd call soon. On the drive home, I wasn't so sure about making that call again. The problem was that even though I liked Eric, I loved Honey.

Maybe my timing just wasn't right, and the one thing that I was sure of now was that my love for Honey couldn't be washed away by another nigga's dick.

I kept driving in thought, and looked at my phone to see if Mama had called back. She had called twice. It was too early in the morning to call her, but I did anyway. She answered the phone, hissing at me.

"Bitch, this better be real good. Holla," she said.

"Where is Shania and Honey at?" I asked.

"At Disney World."

"Mama, quit playin'. Where are they?"

"Shania is asleep, but I haven't seen Honey since yesterday. I thought he was there with you."

My heart dropped to my stomach. "I spoke to him earlier, and I thought he told me he was at yo' crib. He said you, Trice, and Shania was at the store."

"Well, he lied. He probably hemmed up somewhere with one of his bitches, and like always, he'll be home soon. So don't call me panicking, especially when you've made your choice to stay with that nigga. Tell him I'ma kick his ass for lying on me. For now, I'm taking my ass back to sleep."

Mama hung up on me. I was so worried about where Honey was. It didn't dawn on me that he was at home until I stuck the key in the door and the smell of marijuana hit me. I touched the light switch to turn on the light, but it didn't come on. The house was almost pitch black, and as I tiptoed my way forward to the great room, I could see Honey chilling back on the couch, smoking Kush. Even that room was dark and all I could see clearly was the white part of his eyes.

"Where have you been?" he asked.

"I went out with Simone. The club was boring as fuck, so I drove around for a while and then came home. I thought you were still in Cali. When I talked to Mama, she said you left yesterday. Why didn't you bring Shania home with you? I thought she was comin' back with you."

Honey turned on the seventy-two inch TV that was mounted into the wall. The brightness from the TV gave the room a sliver of more light. He looked me over and his fire-red eyes stopped right at my pussy. He took another hit from the joint and blew smoke into the air.

"I didn't bring Shania home with me because I had a feeling that when I got here, I was gon' have to beat yo' muthafuckin' ass. The last thing I wanted was for her to witness that shit."

The best thing that I could do right now was stay quiet and let this situation calm itself. Honey had a look in his eyes that I hadn't seen before, and even though he'd threatened to kick my ass, he had never done it.

I walked off, but before I made it to the kitchen, Honey rushed up from behind me and grabbed the back of my shirt, pulling me to him. He wrapped his arm around my neck and squeezed so I couldn't move. He placed his lips close to my ear and spoke through gritted teeth. I could smell the alcohol and weed on his breath.

"I'ma ask yo' ass again, and this time, I want the truth. Where in the fuck have you been?"

I reached for his arm, trying to move it away from my neck, but his grip was too tight. "I already told you! And just so you know, you're hurtin' me. Your grip is too tight!"

Honey released his arm. "Hurt you? Naw, I haven't hurt you yet."

I turned around, and was met with his tightened fist that cracked me right in the face. My eyes fluttered, my vision blurred, and a flash of darkness came across the room. My whole body went limp, and I crashed so hard to the floor, hitting my head. Honey stood over me and pulled me up by my shirt. "Whenever you're ready to tell me, I'm listening, Karrine."

I was so stunned that he'd hit me. Through a nearly shut eye, I looked at him. Tears rolled down my face, but he didn't appear to have any sympathy for me. Since I didn't answer his question, he punched me again, causing my head to jerk back. This time, my nose stung and started to bleed. I could taste the blood as it ran over my puffy lips and into my mouth.

"Why . . . why are you doin' this to me?" I cried out as Honey held me in his hands, shaking the shit out of me.

"Because you played me, bitch! I told you what was gon' happen if you played me, didn't I? Now, tell me where you've been before I kick my goddamn foot in your throat!"

I didn't doubt that he would do it, so I quickly spoke up. "I . . . I was with Eric. I spent most of the night with him."

"Did you fuck him? Or do I have to remove your clothes and find that shit out for myself? I can already smell that nigga's cheap-ass cologne all over you. Did you do it?"

I slowly nodded and separated my bloody, cracked mouth to speak. By then, though, Honey shoved me backward and let me go. My head hit the floor again and he got up. He walked away from me and went into his office, slamming the door behind him.

Barely able to see, I got off the floor and staggered upstairs to our bedroom with one shoe on and one off. I went into the bathroom to clean myself up. As I looked at my swollen, bruised eye in the mirror, I touched my face and it was numb. Blood stained my shirt, and my nose was still gushing blood. Trying to stop it, I pinched my nose and tilted my head back. I could taste the blood rushing down my throat and I spit it into the sink. I splashed water all over my face then I patted it with a towel. I glared at the mirror again, hating myself and wanting so badly to kill Honey for what he'd done to me. My thoughts were all over the place. I left the bathroom, and went into the bedroom to retrieve a gun from underneath the mattress. I limped back down the stairs, and when I pushed on the door to Honey's office it squeaked open.

Honey had his head down on his desk. When he lifted it, I aimed the gun right at him. He held his hands out and gazed at me with an intense stare.

"If you hate me that much," he said in a calm tone. "Do it. This is your second attempt to take my life, and I'll be so glad when you get exactly what you want. I'm not it, ma. I'm not the nigga you're looking for, and if it's gotten to the point where you want to kill me then you need to free yourself of me. Do it now, Karrine, and let's get this shit over with."

A slow drip of blood started to run from my nose again. It dripped over my lips, along with my flowing, salty tears. The gun trembled in my shaking hands, and when I squeezed the trigger, all the gun did was click. I squeezed it again and again . . . click, click, click. No bullets were inside of it, and yet again, I was fucked. When Honey got out of his seat, I threw the gun at him. He ducked and the gun hit the wall.

As he approached me, I pounded his chest with my fists and clawed my nails down the side of his face, scratching it.

"I . . . I hate you!" I yelled out. "I hate you so damn much, Honey, I swear I do!"

"No, you don't," he said, trying to embrace me and get me to calm down.

I kept pulling away from him, but he had a tight grip on my arms. He held them steady and looked into my watered down eyes. "If you thought I would ever have you in a house with loaded guns, you got me fucked up. I knew you would try this shit on me again, but why did you make me do this to you, Karrine? I never wanted to hurt you like this, and if you were that damn unhappy with me, why didn't you just leave me? You don't have to stay with me if you don't want to. If you want me to free you so you can be with another nigga, all you gotta do is say so. What else can I do, ma, but threaten you. You . . . you fucked with my head and made me hurt you like this. I'm sorry for that shit and—"

Honey let me go and he swung around to face the wall, trying to hide his emotions. I stood still, attempting to shake my cries that left me unable to catch my breath.

"Don't you dare blame this on me! You didn't have to hit me, and all of this revolves around yo' ongoin' disrespect! I went to go see Eric because I wanted to try somethin' different. What I found out was I was wastin' my time, because the whole time he was inside of me, all I could think about was you! I felt guilty, and I knew the shit would hurt you if you found out about it. I left Eric's crib tellin' myself that my love for you was so strong that I just had to deal with whatever, until this shit got better. But tell me this, Honey? When you're out fuckin' with all of those bitches, do you think about me? Do you ride home feelin' guilty and shed tears when your dick is far up in those bitches pussies? I don't think so, and how dare you stand there and act like I had no right to do what I did. How dare you beat my ass like I'm the one who should've known better. You were wrong on so many different levels, and you can take that sorry you just offered me and shove it up yo' black ass!"

I turned to walk away, but Honey came up from behind and eased his arms around my waist. "Damn, I fucked up, all right. I'm real sorry and don't you know I love you, ma? Those bitches don't mean shit to me. I do feel guilty about that shit, you just don't know how guilty. But this ain't about them. It's about you fucking with another nigga. Didn't you know what that shit would do to me? I was going crazy sitting here waiting for you and knowing that he probably had his dick in you. That shit didn't work for me, and I told you before that it wouldn't."

I removed his arms from around me and turned to face him. He stared at my nearly shut eye and reached out his hand to touch it.

"Deal with it like I do, Honey. And if you felt guilty you would've stopped the bullshit a long time ago. And just so you know, you haven't been the only one doin' your homework. I have too, startin' with the week before you went to Cali. Monday you were at Kita's house fuckin' her, on Tuesday you were at dinner with that white chick, then you took her to a fancy hotel and screwed her. I didn't see you until Wednesday afternoon, and when you brought yo' hot-dick ass up in here, you put yo' dick up in me and dug for gold like I was the best thing ever. Thursday was your rest day, but by Friday, nigga, you were hyped again. I believe Champagne was her name, and you fucked her in the backseat of your truck. Saturday was all about business, but Sunday the ho in you came out again. I guess Kita needed her pussy sucked again, and that didn't satisfy you enough, because you came here and dined on me for several hours. Now, tell me this, Honey. How much pussy does one man need? How much bullshit do you expect me to put up with—and realistically, shouldn't you be the one with a fucked up face like this, instead of me?"

Honey was speechless. All he could do was turn away from me.

"Yeah, that's what I thought," I said. "Sit on that shit for a while, nigga, and if you can come up with a legitimate reason as to why I should stay with yo' ass, let me know. That love shit you talkin' ain't good enough, so let me know what else you come up with within the next several hours. That's when I'll be gettin' my borin' ass the fuck out of here and leavin' yo' ass at peace."

I went upstairs to our bedroom and started packing. The only place I really wanted to go was to Cali with Mama, but I wasn't so sure if she wanted me there on a full-time basis.

Hopefully, with Shania being there, Mama would feel good about it. I just didn't know right now, and what I intended to do was show up with some of my things now and send for some later.

By seven o'clock in the morning, I was done stuffing three suitcases and putting some of my things in a duffle bag. I carried my suitcases to the front door, and I could see Honey sitting quietly on the couch, finishing a joint. His shirt was off and his jeans were hanging off his ass, showing his Calvin Klein briefs.

As I pulled the heavy duffle bag down the steps, he called my name. I didn't go see what he wanted until I dropped the bag at the door.

"What?" I said with a white bandage covering my eye. My face was so fucked up that I wouldn't dare walk out in public with it not being covered up.

"What is it that you want from me?" he asked. "I'm not really understanding it, and you have never really made yourself clear."

"What I want—or wanted—you have never been willin' to give. And if I didn't make myself clear, you can now take all the time you need to figure out what I was tryin' to say. Until then, I'll be with our daughter."

I left having no regrets, and I felt good about my decision to move the fuck on.


My suitcases and bags were in the car, so I stopped at the bank to clear my account out, just in case, then caught a plane, heading to Cali with Mama. I didn't tell her I was coming, and when Trice opened the door for me, she looked at my face and gasped.

"Don't even ask," I said, strolling in with some of my suitcases. The taxi driver had the rest of them, and he placed them in the foyer. After I paid him, he left.

"Where is Mama at?"

"She's in the kitchen with Shania."

I headed toward the kitchen, watching from a far as Mama gazed out of the large picture windows that viewed the lavish backyard. Shania was on her hip and Mama swayed back and forth while singing to her. Shania smiled and pulled on Mama's long braids. I cleared my throat, and when Shania reached out, Mama turned around.

"Hey pretty girl," I said to Shania who Mama had handed over to me. She stared at me and swallowed hard.

"Car accident?" she questioned.

"No," I replied.

"You ran into the wall?"

"Nope."

"Fell off a bike?"

"Haven't been on one in years."

Mama looked over my shoulder at Trice. "Come get Shania while Karrine and I have a talk."

Trice came into the kitchen and got Shania, who fussed because she didn't want to let me go.

"Let's go fix up your dollhouse," Trice said. "Do you want to go do that?"

Shania smiled and left with Trice. Mama told me to sit at the table, so I did. She lit a cigarette, and after several deep puffs, she sat down at the table with me.

"If you're here for me to feel sorry for you, I must tell you that I don't. I knew this day was coming, Karrine, and I don't know why you're here because all you're going to do is keep on running back to his ass."

"No, I'm not. I'm done. I swear I'm done."

"You won't be done until you have to put a bullet in that nigga's head. And it's gon' be a damn shame, too, because not only will I lose out, but Shania will too. If you and Honey had listened to me from the beginning, we wouldn't even be here. I told you I didn't want to be in the middle of this, now you got me so damn mad that I don't know what to do."

"I know now that I should have listened, but it's so hard, Mama, especially when you love somebody and—"

"Love," Mama shouted. "Don't talk to me about love. Who you need to be in love with is your fucking self. If you did love yourself, you wouldn't have ever allowed Honey to get away with all of that dumb shit he was doing. You knew what kind of nigga he was, Karrine, and what did you do? You ran off and had a damn baby with him. You still around here fucking his ass, and you could be pregnant right now and wouldn't even know it. I taught you better than this, didn't I? Please tell me that I didn't raise a goddamn fool."

Mama's words stung, but what else did I expect her to say?

"Sooo, I slipped, fell, and bumped my head. Just like we all do sometimes, but I'm gon' bounce back and redeem myself."

"Don't talk about it, be about it. And whenever that nigga comes here, because you know he will, you don't need to be redeeming yourself with his dick in your mouth or in your pussy."

Mama got up and removed the bandage from my eye. She looked at it and shook her head with disgust. She then sat back at the table and reached for the cell phone in her pocket. After calling Honey, she put the phone on speakerphone.

"I knew this call was coming," he said nonchalantly. "What's up?"

"You mean what's going down? Yo' ass is, if I ever have to see Karrine's face like this again. I can't believe you did this shit, Honey, and when you hurt her, nigga, don't you know you hurt me too?"

"It was an accident, and I failed to control myself. I apologized to her and now I'm apologizing to you. After this, I don't want to talk about this shit no more. When you call me, only call to talk about business, not about my relationship with Karrine."

Honey hung up on Mama and her eyes grew wide. She threw a fit and called him all kinds of names as she called him back. To no surprise, he didn't answer. That didn't stop her from leaving him a message.

"You black ass son of a bitch," Mama shouted into the phone. "If I could, I would get up from here and come beat yo' ass! And if you don't remember nothing else, you had better remember this. Never bite the hand that feeds you, nigga, do you hear me? Get yo' mind right, and within the hour, I expect a phone call from you, and you better have plenty of regrets! Plenty!"

Mama ended the call. Twenty minutes later, Honey called back. She stormed off into another room to talk to him. When she came back, her lips were poked out and she had much attitude.

"I can't believe y'all got me caught up in this foolishness. While I do not think Honey is a bad person, Karrine, all I will say is that he's not for you. I'ma leave it there, then I'm going to ask, why are your suitcases sitting at my front door?"

I got up from my chair and went to go rest my head on Mama's shoulder to calm her.

"Because, Mommy, me and Shania wanted to know if we could stay here with you for a while. I promise you that we won't be no trouble at all and I'll be on my best behavior."

Mama moved my head off her shoulder. "Shania won't be no trouble, but I don't know about you. With all the money that you have, why can't you go find your own place? I'm getting sick of you and your sisters. All y'all do is come here and call every day, talking about y'all problems. Do y'all know what it's like to live a drama-free life? Damn!"

"I'm tryin' to live one right now, and the only reason I don't feel as though I should go get my own place right now is because look at all the money I can save for Shania, living here with you. You got this big ole six bedroom house, over here living like a movie star and getting paid while chilling back. Plus, I know how much you like to have Shania here—"

"Karrine, stop right there and get out of my face. I'll let you know what's up in a few hours, but for now, it's not looking good for you."

Mama walked away, but I already suspected that she wanted me to stay. This was just how her life was supposed to be, and she knew it. She never got back to me about staying with her, but almost three weeks later, I was still there. Chilling by the poolside and listening to music on my headsets. I was flipping through a magazine when I looked up and saw Honey heading my way. He rocked a white wife-beater and some cargo shorts. A bandana was tied around his locs, and my heart raced as our eyes stayed locked together. He came up and stood in front of me.

"Come home," he said. "Please. I miss you, ma, and the reason why you should be there is because I love you, and you have my word that I will cease all the dumb shit and do right by you. I will never put my hands on you again, and I'll make our home the most peaceful place ever. All I need is for you to trust me on this, please. Trust me."

My heart was pounding fast. I blinked away the tears that were trying to escape from my eyes. They grew wide when I saw Honey reach into his pocket and pull out a small black box. He opened it and flashed a diamond ring.

"You know I wouldn't do this shit unless I was serious," he said. "I'm dead serious, so let's do this shit and stop wasting time listening to muthafuckas who want to dictate our lives and tell us what to do. You know how I feel about you, and vice versa. We're wasting time being apart, and my life just don't feel right without you."

I struggled with this shit. And as much as I talked about Rihanna, I now knew how she'd felt about Chris Brown. Some shit just felt destined, and I found it so hard to let Honey go for good. He dropped down to one knee and I inched closer to him. I reached for the box, gazed at the ring, then closed the box. A tear rolled down my face as I moved my head from side to side and reached out to touch his handsome face.

"As . . . as much as I want to, I can't. You hurt me too bad, Honey, and I will never forgive you for what you did to me. I know exactly how you feel when you say our relationship feels destined, but we're just not good for each other. You very well may make some changes, but I know you, Honey. I know what makes you tick, I know how you like power and control, and there are plenty of bitches out there who will allow you to have that and then some. I . . . I just can't do it, baby, so we need to pack up our feelings for each other and move the fuck on."

Honey looked down at the ground then he shifted his eyes back to me. "Is that what you really want? If there are no doubts whatsoever in yo' head, then I'll check out of here and deal with your decision. But if you have an inkling of a doubt, I want you to be real with yourself and come back home with me. So, what's the verdict? Because when I walk, I'm walking for good."

I did have doubts, but I was sticking to what I'd said. Still, I inched forward and gave Honey a long, wet, and juicy kiss. The feel of his hands around my waist made me want him so badly, but I backed away.

"Good-bye, Honey. Go do you, and Shania and me will see you whenever you come to visit."

Honey wiped his lips, swallowed hard and nodded his head. He stood up, and before he walked away, I eased the black box back into his pocket. He stared at me for a few more seconds, then walked away. I rested back on the lounging chair and released a deep sigh as he faded out of my sight. I wasn't sure if I had done the right thing or not, but something inside of me felt real good. I was pleased to show Mama that she hadn't raised a complete damn fool, and it was good to know that Honey and I wouldn't repeat the cycle that Mama and Ray had set before us. For now, it was good-bye and certainly good riddance to the only nigga I ever really loved.

I realized that in life, sometimes, you have to fall and bump your head hard, before you begin to see certain things for what they really are. You also have to step back from a situation, just to get a clear picture of it. That was what I did pertaining to the situation between Honey and me. I stepped back and let the shit do what it was going to do. I attempted to set Honey free, and even though turning down his proposal hurt me like hell, I had to turn it down, because Honey was in no position to marry anyone. He was still fucked up in the head, and he wanted control over everything, including me. His business dealings with Mama were his priority, and he made it clear that Shania and I would always come second. To me, we weren't even second.

Needless to say, that didn't work for me. I needed much more than a nigga who put making paper before me, and I needed more than a dick-happy fool who thought it was okay to run from one bitch to the next. I had put up with that mess for long enough. Now it was my time to shine. It was time to do me and let Honey do him. Allowing him to do him meant that I had to keep my mouth shut whenever he brought other bitches around. I had to silence myself when he spoke to them over the phone, and when Mama contacted him to do "special" duties for her, I couldn't say shit. Not to her, or to him. Basically, I pretended as if everything was all good, when in reality it wasn't.

The reason why it wasn't, was because I still loved Honey. He was Shania's father, and I wanted him to get his shit together. I wanted good things to fall into his lap, but with all of the crooked shit he had been doing, I expected setbacks for him that would cost him dearly.

All that shoot-'em-up shit needed to cease. Honey had gotten ruthless, and there was a time when he wouldn't get down like that. He would let other niggas do the dirty work, but since Mama had been shot Honey had been on a roll. I was worried about him. He seemed to be moving in a different direction, and it made me crazy.

Today was Shania's birthday. I was in the kitchen at Honey's crib cooking breakfast. The only reason I was there was because the party was scheduled to be at his place. Mama came with me, and we had gotten in from California late last night.

Mama and me had been getting along well. I stayed out of her way, and she stayed out of mine. I never got into her business deals with Honey, and even though I disagreed with what had been going on, I figured that my gripes would go in one ear and out the other. Neither of them were about to stop anything because of me. It was all about grown folks making grown folks' decisions, and the only business I had was pertaining to Shania. I wanted her birthday party to be real special. Honey and I, both, had spent a fortune, just to see our baby girl's face light up. She was so excited and it was because of her that I was already awake at six in the morning.

"I know you're excited, little girl, but couldn't you let me sleep a little longer this mornin'?" I spoke to Shania while holding her on my hip, trying to cook at the same time.

"What did I tell you about cooking with that girl in your arms," Mama said as she came up from behind me and removed Shania from my grip. "That's dangerous, Karrine, and she can get burned from being so close to that stove."

"I'm not goin' to burn her, so be quiet. The grits and eggs are on the back burners, and she can't reach them."

"Excuses, excuses," Mama said, walking away to go sit at the kitchen table. "One day you'll learn."

She had the nerve to get on me about cooking with Shania in my arms, but she sat at the table and lit a cigarette with Shania on her lap.

"You need to give Shania back to me right now, because smokin' around her is not a good thing. I know that, and you do too."

Mama blew smoke into the air, away from Shania. "I only needed a few puffs. My nerves are bad and you already know how I feel about coming back to Chicago. The only reason I'm here is because of this birthday party, but I'm out of here on Monday. What about you?"

"I'm out of here, too. There ain't no reason for me to stay, especially not in this house with Honey. I can barely stand to be around him, but today will be an exception."

"You need to stop lying to yourself about that nigga, Karrine. You know you still love his dirty drawers, and if he got his shit together you would invite him right back into the pussy."

"Keepin' it real, maybe so. But that's the problem. He will never get his act together, so there ain't no need for me to keep hopin' and dreamin' that he will."

Mama smashed her cigarette in the ashtray and started to bounce Shania on her lap. Shania was cracking up, and she kept hugging Mama and pulling on her long braids.

"Girl, let my hair go," Mama said. "I can already tell that you're going to be snatching bitches up by their hair and yanking their asses around like ragdolls. You's a gangsta baby, and granny sho-nuff loves her little gangsta boo, too."

I quickly scrambled the eggs, feeling very annoyed by what Mama had said. "Don't say that to her, Mama. She ain't no gangsta baby, and I'm not goin' to teach her to get down like we do. Or should I say did, because that ain't happenin' anymore."

"Since when?" Mama challenged. "Didn't you just shoot up a nigga several months ago, outside of a club? I mean, correct me if I'm wrong, but Shania's Mama and Daddy ain't representing a pastor or the first lady at a church, are y'all?"

"No, and I'm glad we're not, because they have way more shit goin' on than we do. And no matter what we're representin', I don't want Shania to go down the same path as I did."

"What was so wrong with your path? I hate for a spoon-fed bitch who had any and everything she always wanted to complain about shit later on in life. At the end of the day, you and your sisters had it made. You heifers didn't want for nothing, so don't stand there being so ungrateful. Just so I don't have to let my gangsta baby see me put my foot in yo' ass, we're going upstairs. Holla when the food is done, and whatever you do, don't burn my bacon."

I rolled my eyes at Mama as she left the kitchen with Shania. She didn't understand how I wanted things with Shania to be different. It wasn't that I was saying that she was a bad mother. I just didn't want Shania being introduced to the things that I, Chyna, and Simone had been introduced to. It was as simple as that.

Breakfast was ready, but unfortunately, I was the only one at the kitchen table eating. Honey had been gone all night, and he wasn't even home when we got in from California. Mama said that she had spoken to him, but all he said to her was that he would be here to get things ready for the party. It was only seven thirty now, so I suspected he would get here before the party started at three.

With my jean shorts and pink wife beater on, I cut into my pancakes and chewed. I could see my beautiful reflection on the sparkling glass table. I wanted to look nice for Shania's party, so I had my beautician hook up my short layered hair that swooped across my forehead and revealed my makeup free face. My natural beauty was on display, and I was pleased that my daily workout regimen had brought about great results. My body was on point again, and it didn't even look like I'd had a baby. As soon as I heard the front door open, I held my breath and sat up straight in the chair. I figured it was Honey, so I turned my head to look at the TV that was mounted on the wall. I pretended as if I was indulged, and I didn't turn my head until I heard his voice.

"Do you want something to eat?" he asked the light-bright bitch, Audrey, who entered the kitchen with him. Her natural hair sat wildly on her head, and she had a slender, model-like frame with minimal curves. This wasn't the first time I had seen her with Honey, and deep down I knew he kept bringing her around to irritate me. But today was not the day to fuck with me. It was

Shania's birthday, not time for him to flaunt his bitches around just to make me jealous.

I cleared my throat and did my best not to show that I was frustrated. "Excuse me, but I didn't make enough food for you and your guest. I made that food for me, Mama, and Shania. They should be comin' downstairs soon to eat."

"Oh, that's fine," Audrey said with a forced smile. "I wasn't hungry anyway."

The bitch looked like she needed something to eat, but it damn sure wouldn't be my food. Honey knew not to play with me, and with Audrey being here, I figured this nigga would do his best to try my patience.

"Are you sure?" he said to her. "I mean, if you're hungry, I can always cook you something."

I almost choked. Nigga please. His ass couldn't cook a hotdog, let alone breakfast. I turned my head again and focused on the TV.

"I'm good, Honey," Audrey said in a proper tone. "All I need is the bathroom so I can go tinkle, and maybe some orange juice or something when I return. Do you think you can handle that for me?"

"Not a problem," Honey said. "And you already know where the bathroom is."

From the corner of my eye, I could see Honey's black Barbie walk away. He came up to me with his hands in the pockets of his faded jeans. His locs were covered with a bandana, and a leather black jacket was over the gray V-neck shirt he wore that tightened on his muscular chest. With a diamond earring in his ear, and dimples coming through with his smile, Honey put the word sexy to shame.

"Why you got an attitude?" he said, picking up my fork. He attempted to put my pancake in his mouth, but I snatched the fork from his hand.

"I don't have an attitude, and please do not put my food or fork in your mouth. Ain't no tellin' where it's been."

"I can't tell you where it's been, but I can tell you where I would like for it to be."

"Not interested. But if you want to tell me somethin', tell me this. Why would you bring your tramp here on Shania's birthday? I hope Audrey ain't gon' be here all day, is she?"

"As a matter of fact, she is. I invited her and her nephew to come because Audrey likes Shania and Shania likes her. She also bought a nice present for Shania, and Audrey would like to give it to her. You don't have a problem with that, do you?"

I did, but he wouldn't know it. "I don't have a problem with that, Honey, so do you. Have hella fun today, and please keep in mind that today is about Shania, not about me and you."

I got up from the table to walk away. Honey reached out and grabbed a healthy chunk of my ass, squeezing it. I swung around and pointed my finger near his face. "Don't play with me, nigga. I'm not your toy, and those days are long gone. My wish is that you start to recognize that and stop playin' these childish games that, in the long run, will only hurt you."

The smirk on Honey's face was enough to make my damn blood boil. I hated that he could see right through me. I was determined to make him think that I didn't care about him anymore. He walked up and stood inches in front of me, leaving little breathing room between us.

"Like always," he said in a whisper. "It's good seeing you, Karrine, and I'm glad you're back home where you belong. All you ever have to do is say the word and this shit will be back on and popping with us again. You got the power, ma. Use it to your advantage and stop wasting all this unnecessary time."

Honey leaned in to kiss me, but I quickly turned my head. That was when Audrey came into the kitchen with her arms folded.

"Really?" she said, looking at Honey. She didn't dare confront me, and all I did was walk away from them. "Did you just try to kiss her?"

"If I did," Honey said nonchalantly. "So what? Don't confront me over no bullshit in my own crib. If you got a problem with what you just saw, remember, you do have options."

I shook my head on the way upstairs. Better her than me, I thought. I was glad it was her dealing with his shit, instead of me.

Several hours later, Shania's birthday party had gotten started. The backyard was packed with kids running around, trying to get on the carousel, ride the pony, jump in the balls, get their faces painted, watch the clown, or eat hotdogs and hamburgers that Honey had cooking on the grill.

For the first hour, Shania was having a blast playing with the other kids. But after the face painter painted her face, that was it for Shania. She got sleepy and was very irritable. She was afraid of the clown, and after crying so much, she winded up falling asleep in Honey's arms. He carried her upstairs to her bedroom, and returned moments later without her.

"I have Mama to thank for all that noise right there," Honey said, looking at Mama as she sat at the picnic table, smoking a cigarette and drinking beer. She seemed to be in a bad mood, and was going off on everybody who said something to her.

"No, you have yourself and Karrine to thank for gangsta baby. I'm the only one who knows how to get control over her, and the two of y'all let her do whatever."

Honey couldn't say shit, because he truly had Shania spoiled rotten. Mama did too, but I wasn't about to call her out on anything right now. She kept wincing at Chyna's man, Desmon, and Honey's bitch, Audrey, wasn't getting much play either. She was running around in the backyard with her nephew that Honey invited. That kept her away from Honey for a while, but every now and then she would look at us to see what we were up to. That would be nothing, because Shania had kept me so busy today that I didn't have time to trip off Honey. He had been barbecuing for past hour or so, and while the kids ate hotdogs and hamburgers, the adults had saucy ribs and chicken. I had to give it up to him—the food was pretty good.

Chyna and Desmon were standing near the carousel watching his niece. They looked good together, but I could tell by the look in Mama's eyes that she wasn't pleased. Simone was inside talking to someone on her cell phone, and when she came outside she walked up to Honey with a paper plate in her hand.

"I'll take some chicken, a hotdog, and a hamburger. Make sure my hotdog is as black as you, and I would like extra barbecue sauce."

Honey and Simone never really got along, but he piled the food high on her plate without saying anything harsh to her. "Extra sauce can be found on the picnic table over there, and the buns are over there too."

Simone didn't bother to thank him, and I heard him whisper "ungrateful bitch" under his breath.

She heard it too, and quickly turned around. "Yo' Mama, bastard. How about that?"

Mama slammed her hand on the table. "How about you leave me out of the bullshit and get yo' nappy-head ass somewhere and sit down?"

Simone was working the natural look too. She rocked all brand-name clothes, and the Jimmy Choo pumps she had on had to cost a fortune. Nobody was surprised that Simone was still doing video porn, but if that was how she wanted to get down, so be it.

"Excuse me," Simone said, putting her hand on her hip and addressing Mama. "I was talkin' to Honey, not you. You always tryin' to take up for him, and every time somebody got somethin' to say to that nigga you come runnin' to his defense."

Mama pursed her lips and she threw her hand back at Simone. "Don't feed me that bullshit, Simone. Yo' ass the one who threw me under the bus, and the only person I was defending was myself."

Simone rolled her eyes and walked over to the picnic table to get her sauce, buns, and potato salad. Honey came over to us and kissed Mama on her cheek. That surely made her smile, and it was no secret to any of us that Honey was Mama's favorite.

"Are you gon' eat something or not?" he said to her. "If so, you'd better get on it now, because the food is starting to fade by the minute."

"Nah, I'm not gon' eat right now. I got too much on my mind."

Honey looked at me. I turned my head and all he did was laugh and walk away. *Bastard,* I thought. Ugh, I hated him, but still loved him to death. All I could do was laugh to myself about how confused I was.

Honey made his way over to Audrey, who was watching her nephew ride a pony. I guess they settled their dispute from earlier, because the bitch was now smiling. She wrapped her arms around him and looked over his shoulder to see if I was watching. I turned my attention to Simone who had sat at the table with me and Mama.

"Nice party," Simone said. "Too bad the birthday girl ain't enjoyin' it, but at least you'll have a whole lot of pictures to show her when she gets older." Simone held up her phone and put her face next to Mama's, taking a picture. We laughed, but Mama didn't even smile. Simone elbowed Mama in her side. "What's wrong with you, old lady? Why you actin' all funny and stuff?"

Mama sipped from her can of beer and evil-eyed Desmon and Chyna. "Nothing. There's nothing wrong with me—I'm just ready to go back home."

"I thank you for comin' to Shania's party, and if you want to leave you can," I said.

"When I leave, gangsta baby goin' with me," Mama said as a matter of fact. "You can stay and play all you want to, but peace awaits us back at home."

Simone looked around the backyard at all the kids happily playing. "Peace?" Simone said. "This birthday party is drama free, and the only drama that may come about will be between you and me, when I ask why you called me a nappy-head bitch. Are you sayin' that you don't like my new style?"

Mama looked at Simone's hair that was shaped into a wild, nappy afro. To me, it was cute, and I got tired of seeing Simone with long weaved-in hair.

"I do like your new style," Mama said. "But the shit is real nappy. Why you got it so nappy? Maybe you need to spray some of that Afro Sheen shit in it, just to give it some shine. It needs some shine and—"

Mama stopped talking when Chyna and Desmon came up to the table. Desmon was dressed preppy in a Nike outfit and cap. He looked like he was on his way to play golf, rather than being at a child's birthday party. Chyna was in a simple, strapless sundress that cut right above her knees. Her long braids looked freshly done, and they were pulled back to show the roundness and beauty of her smooth, chocolate face.

"Jazel is having a wonderful time," Desmon said to me. "Thanks for inviting us, and it's been such a pleasure watching Chyna do her thing with Jazel. One day she's going to make a great mother, and I can't wait for that day to happen."

Chyna blushed. Simone and me smiled, but Mama gagged. She coughed and covered her mouth as if she was choking on something. Simone reached over to pat her back. "Mama, are you okay?" she said. "Are you chokin'?"

Mama squeezed her watered down eyes and cleared her throat. She swallowed, then looked at Chyna. "All I can say is good luck with that. If you wouldn't mind getting me a bottle of water, I will shut my mouth and stay calm like you asked me to."

I wasn't sure what all of that was about, but Chyna went over to the cooler to get Mama's water. Desmon excused himself and said that he needed to go to the bathroom. When Chyna came back, she gave the bottle of water to Mama.

"You know you's a fool," she said to Mama. "When all is said and done, Desmon is nice, and he's my soul mate."

"No," Mama said, removing the cap from the bottle. "When all is said and done, Desmon is married and he will never divorce his wife. He's using you for sex, he's paying you for your pussy, and when he gets tired of you he will dump you and move on to the next dumb bitch. Aside from that, I said it once and I'll say it again. A thug is the one to love. Most of them will provide for you like no other, he will protect you, he will have yo' damn back, and you don't have to worry about him committing suicide because of his struggles. He has a strong backbone like no other, but that wimpy-ass nigga you've been wasting your time with is too weak. If his money goes, so does he and so do you. I'm just warning you, Chyna, and yet again, you sure do know how to pick them."

Simone and me didn't say a word. Obviously Mama and Chyna had had this conversation before. That was why Mama seemed pissed, but as with all of us, Mama needed to let go and let us make our own decisions, good or bad.

Chyna didn't bother to respond to Mama. She went inside to find Desmon.

"I'm going inside to go check on gangsta baby," Mama said. "Maybe I can talk some sense into her, because I damn sure can't talk no sense into y'all."

I stopped Mama before she got out of her seat. "She's still sleepin', Mama, and I have the monitor right here next to me. If I hear her, I'll go get her. For now, you need to chill. I don't know why you're so upset, and we're supposed to be here having a good time today, ain't we?"

"I am having a good time," Mama said. "But it's hard to sit here and pretend that everything is all good, Karrine. Chyna around here flaunting around another woman's husband as if he belongs to her; you still playing the sucker role for Honey; and Simone has now settled for hardcore porn with the nutty professor. So, no, I'm not happy right now. I wish that y'all would do better. I thought that if I pulled myself away from y'all that things would get better. I'm not seeing progress, and if you want to impress me, I need to see some for-real changes being made."

I didn't know where to start with Mama, but it was the wrong time for her to come down on us about all of this stuff. Simone was ready to get into Mama's shit, but when we both saw a prissy bitch come into the yard with Chanel sunglasses shielding her eyes, our attention turned to her. She glanced around the yard as if she were looking for someone. I knew I hadn't invited her to the party, but maybe she was someone who knew Honey.

She looked in his direction, but he didn't appear to be the one she was searching for.

"Who is that bitch?" Simone said with a twisted face.

Mama sucked her teeth and reached for her beer. "You'll soon see. Pay attention, bitches. This shit is about to get real interesting."

I was confused, but everything became clearer to me when Chyna and Desmon came outside together. The woman charged our way with a mean mug on her face. Once she reached the patio, she removed her shades and rushed up to Desmon, smacking the shit out of him. Chyna backed a few inches away, while Desmon grabbed the woman's hand as she attempted to smack him again.

"Wha . . . what in the hell is your problem?" he shouted to her. "Are you serious, Marva? You couldn't wait until I got home?"

"Hell, no, I couldn't wait, and I don't give a damn where I find you! I told you that if I caught you with this bitch one more time that there will be trouble! Didn't I?"

As we all looked on, embarrassment covered Desmon's face. He tried to pull his wife away from everyone, but she snatched away from him and kept on crying out for a resolution to their madness. "You told me it was over," she tearfully shouted. "You said that you were done with this bitch! Why do you keep lying to me, and when will the lies ever stop?"

Chyna folded her arms and released a deep sigh. "Just so you know," she said to the woman. "You're on bitch number two. By the time you reach three, some shit that you may not appreciate gon' pop off."

"Out!" Desmon said, shoving his wife away. By now, though, many people had stopped what they were doing and were watching the scene unfold. Honey rushed up to the patio, trying to see what was up.

"What's shaking?" he asked.

"My wife was just leaving," Desmon said, following another shove to his wife's shoulder.

His wife, however, wasn't having it. She karate kicked his ass right in the nuts and then hit him across the head with her purse. Desmon grabbed his dick and dropped to his knees. That was when she rushed around him and stormed up to Chyna. Unfortunately, that was the wrong move. Mama was already on her feet and so was Simone. Both of them had their guns aimed directly at the woman's face. She stopped dead in her tracks and stood still as if cement covered her.

"One more step, one more word, one more move, and you's a dead bitch," Mama said. "On the count of three, you gon' turn yo' ass around and slowly exit the premises. We're all going to pretend that this little incident didn't happen, and any issues or concerns that you have with your slick-ass husband will need to be done on his time and his premises, not mine."

"One," Simone said.

The woman released the deep breath she was holding and slowly exited. All eyes were still on her, but you best believe that some of the parents had gotten their kids the fuck out of there.

"Two."

The woman picked up speed as she made her way to the gate. And by the time Simone reached "Three" the bitch was gone. Desmon stood and squeezed his eyes as if he were still in pain.

"I am so sorry about this," he said, looking at all of us. We all had blank expressions on our faces. "I . . . I don't know what got into her, and she—"

Mama was so mad that she didn't bother to hold back. "Get yo' punk-ass out of here," she hissed. "No explanation is needed, because some of us around here already know what yo' ass is already about."

Desmon defended himself. "No . . . no, it's not really like that. My wife and I—"

Mama lifted her hand with the gun in it and aimed it at him. "One," she said.

"Man, you'd better jet," Honey said, walking up to Desmon. "Especially if you don't want your brains splattered on this concrete."

"Two."

Chyna rushed up to Desmon and pulled on his arm. "This is ridiculous," she fussed and rolled her eyes at Mama. "Come on, let's go." She pulled on Desmon's arm and they left together.

I stood in awe and couldn't believe this shit was going down at Shania's birthday party. It wasn't long before everybody checked out of there. Honey and I were both left speechless as our friends, neighbors, and families exited.

Honey's friend, Dingo, walked up to him and gave him five. "Man, y'all need to have this shit on lock, especially with all these kids around. That wasn't a good look."

"You damn right it wasn't," his girlfriend said, holding her daughter's hand. "This shit is crazy."

I didn't bother to comment. It was crazy, but she made sure her daughter left with three of the goody bags in her hand. I walked away, and rolled my eyes at Audrey, who appeared to be shocked by the incident too. When I went inside, Mama was sitting on the couch in the living room, flipping through a magazine. She acted as if nothing happened. I guess I couldn't blame her for standing up for Chyna.

"I'm staying at a hotel tonight," Mama said. "And I'm going back to Cali in the morning. Like I said earlier, Shania is goin' with me. Are you?"

"I'm leaving on Monday. I don't care if you take Shania with you, but do me a favor, okay Mama? Stop tryin' to live our lives for us. Stop interferin', and allow us to do what we wish. You don't have to keep stressin' yourself out like this, and one of these days we'll all have to get our acts together."

"I hope so, because I'm tired of putting myself out there like this. Chyna knows she's in a fucked up situation, so why keep fucking with that fool? You too, Karrine. You know damn well that you haven't put this shit with Honey to rest. I'm not going to keep talking about it, but after today, it will be a long time before I come back to Chicago. Y'all can have this shit for real."

Within the hour, Mama had gathered her things and was ready to go. She carried Shania in her arms who was eating a piece of her birthday cake that never got cut.

"See you soon, precious," I said as I walked with them to the car. I gave Shania a kiss and watched as Honey put Mama's belongings into the car.

"Call me when you get to the hotel," Honey said to Mama. "Unfortunately, I got some heat swinging my way that I need to tell you about. I know you don't want to hear about it right now, but it is what it is."

"No, it is what it is because you haven't been listening to me. I know what you've been doing, and don't blame me when all those chickens come home to roost. Maybe I'll call you when I get home, but if I don't, don't take it personal. Tonight I need some rest, and I want to make sure my gangsta baby enjoys the rest of her birthday."

Honey appeared frustrated, too. He walked off and went back into the house. I was left out in the cold about so much, but it was apparent that Honey had been doing some things that Mama didn't approve of.

I strapped Shania in the car seat and waved at her as Mama backed out of the driveway. The house was a mess, as well as the backyard. Simone said that she would stay to help us clean up, but as we stood in the kitchen, I told her that Honey and I would do it.

"If you insist," she said, sliding lip gloss across her lips. "Besides, I have something to get into tonight. I definitely don't want to be late."

"Late for what? And what did Mama mean when she mentioned you and the nutty professor doin' porn?"

"First of all, Mama needs to mind her own business. She believes that I'm indulged in porn movies with the professor. It ain't even like that, and all I've done is add him to the mix, sometimes, when I put on my little shows."

"It's not her business, but you make it her business when you tell her stuff like that. Stop tellin' her what you're doin' and keep whatever it is that you're doin' private. Be safe and know your boundaries with that shit. I guess if you're happy, so am I."

I reached out to hug Simone and she embraced me back.

"I am happy, very happy, doin' what I do. I'm still in school, too, so please don't worry about me. I'm just buildin' my life the way I want to do it, and to whoever don't like it, fuck them."

I felt the same way. I walked Simone to her car, and after she left, I went back inside to see where Honey was. He was in the backyard talking to Audrey. She was standing between his legs as he sat on the picnic table hugging her. Her nephew was jumping in the balls with Honey's friend's son. His friend was talking to one of the neighbors, and they were the only ones left.

I was so jealous as I watched Audrey and Honey laughing and talking. I hated to keep putting myself in these situations with him. I could have left with Mama and Shania, but I hadn't been alone with Honey in quite some time. I had been keeping my distance, and there was a part of me that wanted to know if I had the strength to truly move on without him. It was so hard to ignore my feelings, but I had to keep being fake.

I stayed in the kitchen to clean up. More mess had been created in the backyard, but with everyone running in and out earlier, opening the fridge, and with paper plates and cups lying everywhere, I got busy. I wasn't sure if Audrey was going to stay all night with Honey, but I guess that would be left up to him. I suspected that she wouldn't, especially since her nephew had been dropped off. I was sure she had to take him home, but what if she came back?

Either way, I cleaned and waited. I waited until everyone was gone, and I peeked out of the living room curtains as Honey stood in the driveway by Audrey's car. They kissed, but as they were smacking lips, I saw a car with tinted windows parked several feet away from Honey's crib. The only reason the car alarmed me was because I noticed the window go halfway down and then it went back up. Not knowing what was up, I hurried into Honey's office and pulled a gun from his drawer. I tucked it behind my back, and then I went outside and stood on the porch with my hands in my pockets.

"Honey," I called out to him. "Come here for a minute, please." I hoped that he didn't think I was trying to interfere with him and Audrey. Even though I may have been, I was more concerned about the suspicious car that was parked nearby.

"In a minute," he said, continuing his conversation.

"It's urgent. I need to tell you somethin'. Now."

Honey sighed and Audrey rolled her eyes at me. Her nephew was already in the car, but as soon as she opened the car door, the suspicious car skidded around the corner. The tires screech loudly, causing Honey to rush in my direction.

"Get the fuck in the house," he shouted.

By then, I already had the gun pulled from behind me, aiming it at the speeding car. Honey stood in front of me, blocking me, but all the car did was speed by with the music blasting loudly. No shots were fired. My chest heaved in and out as I watched the car disappear, and Honey was breathing heavy too. He turned his head to look at me with anger locked in his eyes.

"Go inside," he demanded. "I'll be there in a minute."

"No. I'm not goin' inside unless you're comin' with me."

Honey looked at Audrey who had already gotten into her car and slammed the door. It was pretty obvious that Honey was more interested in saving my life than he was in saving hers. Without saying a word, she backed out of the driveway and left. Honey went inside and I followed behind him.

"What's goin' on?" I questioned as I went into his office with him. "What was that all about, and did you know those niggas in that car?"

Honey ignored me. He picked up his phone and sat against the edge of the desk. "Problem," he said to the person on the other end of the phone. "I need for you to check something out for me. A blue Impala, license plate number MJ4, uh. . . ."

"MJ4-03," I paused and then gave him the last number.

He repeated the numbers and then told the person to get back to him ASAP. After that, Honey ended the call and looked at me.

"Why are you still here?" he asked.

"Because I wanted to help you clean up."

He walked past me, leaving his office. "I don't need your help. What I need is for you to get out of here, because, truthfully, I don't want you here."

"I'll leave, but I want you to leave too. You refuse to tell me what's been goin' on with you, but whatever it is, the least you can do is sleep in a safe place. This house ain't safe and it's obvious that somebody is after you."

Honey turned around to face me and snapped. "There are plenty of niggas after me, but so damn what? I'm not living my life in fear, and ain't no muthafucka gon' run me away from home. If you are so anxious to know what's going on with me, I'll tell you what's going on with me. For starters, you are what's going on. You rejected me, and you won't allow me to be with the people in this world who I care about the most. You keep Shania away from me, and you prevent me from being the full-time father that I need to be. You keep telling me to change my ways, but ain't it a fact that you fell in love with me for being the muthafucka you always knew me to be? I'm doing crazy shit right now, ma, 'cause my head ain't on straight. I'm doing away with niggas who making tiny mistakes that can easily be forgiven. But I can't forgive 'cause I'm angry. I'm angry with you, and I'm angry with yo' Mama. She never has time to listen, and I feel like all of this shit is on me. All of it, Karrine, every last bit of it, and a nigga getting tired of the bullshit."

Honey turned to walk away. I stood for a moment, thinking about what he'd said. I knew his plate was full, but there was a perfect solution. He was the one in control of this situation. Not me, and surprisingly, not even Mama.

I went into the kitchen where Honey stood, looking out at the backyard. "Walk away," I said to him. "Let Mama deal with this bullshit and tell her you're done with it. Do you think she'll be upset with you for stepping away from the business? I don't think so, and you need to tell her how you really feel."

"I guess you really don't know your mother too well, Karrine. She would kill me before she'd let me walk away. I'm in so deep that I wouldn't want to leave her with the mess I've created. There are too many niggas involved right now, and when money starts declining because of my absence, a lot of angry people would start to surface."

"So fuckin' what? Bump those niggas. You don't owe nobody shit, and you've done enough for everyone already. One day you're going to have to turn this shit loose. Hopefully that day would come sooner, rather than later."

"The day I turn this shit loose is the day I die. That's just how it is, Karrine, and I gave my word that I'm in until the very end. My loyalty is with Mama, and whether I like this shit or not, it is what it is. As for you," he said, turning around. "What do you want me to do about you? I'm waiting to hear your solution pertaining to that, especially since you seem to have all of the answers right now."

I swallowed the lump in my throat and walked up to Honey with seriousness, as well as truthfulness in my eyes. "My love for you still runs deep, but that doesn't matter right now. I'm fearful of losin' you forever, and the only way for us to ever see where this love can really take us is for you to give all of this up. Your loyalty will have to rest with me, not with Mama. These niggas out here may have to lose in order for me, you, and Shania to gain. I don't want to keep riskin' my life to save yours, and vice versa. And I want you to give me the real respect I truly deserve. You're not there yet, Honey. You're a long way from bein' that kind of nigga, and until you are willin' and able, please don't blame me for the way things are. Much of this is on you, and as I said before, it is within your control."

Honey stared at me. He didn't blink until his phone rang. He then hurried to answer it, and as he wrote something on paper he nodded his head.

"That's what's up. Gather up the crew and meet me there within the hour. I'm on my way."

I watched as Honey quickly changed clothes, tucked his gun down in his jeans and headed for the door. He touched the knob, then turned to face me as I stood with sadness on my face in the foyer.

"Will you be here when I get back?" he asked.

I shook my head. "No. I'll be gone."

Honey shrugged his shoulders and walked out. I said a little prayer, hoping, as always, that I would see or talk to him for at least another day.

# *Chyna*

# 9

At this point, I didn't know who the fuck to be mad at. Desmon, his wife, or at Mama. The whole scene was downright embarrassing, but it wasn't the first time that Marva had confronted us together. The first time was while we were eating dinner at a restaurant. She came in, making a scene. That time the police was called on her, but she fled before they came. The second time was while we were at work. She stormed into Desmon's office, cursing him out and threatening to hurt him if he didn't end this relationship with me. He made it clear that he wasn't going to, and he had to call security to get her to leave.

Today was the third time. She must have been following us, and I didn't appreciate that shit one bit. There I was, trying to prove to my family that Desmon was a decent nigga, but then this bitch showed up acting a goddamn fool.

I wasn't sure how to handle this mess going forward, but this last incident showed me how much I'd changed. There was a time when I would've blown a bitch's brains out for clowning on me like that, but I wasn't trying to go there with Marva. I knew that her marriage with Desmon was over, and I was well aware that he didn't love her anymore. But some bitches didn't want to let go. They wanted to hang on to something that wasn't worth hanging on to. Desmon had already offered her money to keep her "wealthy" status, but the money wasn't enough. She wanted a man who didn't want her, and how stupid was that? He also told her that he wanted a divorce, but the problem was that Desmon had been trying to break her down gently. He was trying to spare her fucking feelings, when realistically he needed to man up and handle this shit so the nonsense would cease. I tried to be patient with the situation, but my patience was running out.

Ashamed about fucking up my niece's birthday party, I picked up the phone to call Karrine and apologize. I figured she was highly upset about what had happened, because if the shoe was on the other foot, and it was my daughter's birthday party, I would be too. When I called her cell phone, I got her voice mail. I left a message, apologizing for what had happened today and told her to relay the message to Honey as well.

Once I ended the call, I went into my living room to watch TV. Desmon said that he was going home to see what the hell was up with his wife, so I didn't want to call and disturb him right now. I was, however, missing him. We had gotten so close, and I knew how much Desmon cared about me. He made me want more out of life, and over the past several months, I felt as if I had truly grown into a better person because of him. My career was on track, money had been flowing and I was doing good without Mama directing my every move.

I still appreciated her, and I enjoyed our daily telephone conversations, but I was still doing me. I kept her informed about some of the things that had been going on with me, Desmon, and his wife, but that was because I wanted Mama to know what was up, just in case something popped off. Desmon's wife didn't come off as being stable to me, so I prepared myself to handle my business with her, if need be.

I had fallen asleep on the couch, and was awakened by a soft knock on my door. I figured it was Desmon stopping by, so I got off the couch and tightened the silk robe around my waist. I yawned before opening the door, and on the other side stood his wife. Her lip was busted and her right eye was nearly closed shut. It was bruised, right along with the side of her face which appeared swollen.

"I . . . I know it's late," she said with tears welled in her eyes. "But can I sit down and talk to you for a moment? Please."

I had some compassion for the bitch, but I had to be sure that she wasn't feeding me no bullshit. "Wait right there," I said, closing my door. I hurried over to the couch and pulled my gun from underneath the pillow. I dropped it into my pocket and then opened the door again.

Marva came in, eyeing her surroundings. My apartment was small, but very cozy and decked out in contemporary furniture. It only had one bedroom, but that was truly enough for me. I invited Marva to sit, and after she sat on the couch, I sat across from her in a chair.

She held her stomach as if it hurt. "I came here to tell you that I'm very sorry about what happened today. None of this is me, and I feel as if I'm losing my mind, trying to chase my husband and get him to do right by me. It's just so hard for me to let go, even though he . . . he beat me like this and told me that he would hurt me again if I confronted you. I don't know what else to do, Chyna. I'm begging you to please let my husband go and let us work on saving our marriage."

"You can't save something that's already dead. And if he beat you like that, why in the hell would you want to still be with him? I don't get it, Marva, and if Desmon doesn't love you anymore then why are you fighting for something that will never be?"

"Because I know he loves me. He's just confused right now, and he always comes back to me when he realizes what he really wants. You . . . you don't know him like I do, and he's going to hurt you too, Chyna. I can guarantee you that if you stay with him, he's going to hurt you too. Both mentally and physically."

"I seriously doubt that, and I'm finding it very hard to believe that the man I know has done all of this to you. How do I know that you didn't beat yourself up, or that you didn't have someone do these things to you, just so you could come here and make your case. Desmon told me how crazy you were, and it's obvious what lengths you will go to, to get him back."

Marva shook her head and wiped a tear that had fallen down her face. "Trust me when I say I'm not the one crazy. He's the one who is crazy, and I feel so foolish for being here and talking to you like this. But I'm here fighting for my family. Maybe counseling is what we need, but I need for you and that other white bitch to back off. I've spoken to her several times about this too, but I haven't had much luck with her. Hopefully I'll have some with you."

Anger swept across my face. I wasn't sure if this heifer was fucking with me or not by bringing up some white bitch. "What white bitch are you talking about? Is she somebody he's supposed to be involved with?"

Marva slowly nodded. "I thought you knew about her, especially since you all work together. She . . . Christina told me that you knew about her and Desmon's relationship, so I thought you knew."

I almost fell back in my chair when she mentioned Christina's name. She was the one who hired me, and there were times when we worked side-by-side together. Marva had to be lying, because Christina didn't even seem to be Desmon's type. She was plain as anything and seemed real timid. Desmon teased her all the time about being so soft spoken, and he encouraged her to be a bit more aggressive, like me.

But the more I sat there thinking about it, my eyes were starting to open. I saw the way Christina lit up when Desmon came into the office every morning. I saw the way she smiled only at him, and there were times when I saw the two of them together at lunch. I never really thought much of it, only because she just didn't seem like his type. But what did I know? I didn't know that he was capable of beating the fuck out of his wife, and could it be possible that I had fucked myself once again?

"Do you know where Desmon is right now?" I asked Marva. "I need to talk to him."

"He left a few hours ago. I thought he was here, but I guess he's with that bitch."

"I take it you know where she lives. If you do, do you mind tellin' me?"

Marva sat silent for a few minutes. She then opened her purse and pulled out a pen and piece of paper. She wrote something on the paper then gave it to me.

"If he's there, tell him that I—"

I quickly stood up and opened the door for Marva to leave. "If he's there, I won't be tellin' him shit, because once I'm done with him, he won't be able to hear me."

Marva walked slowly out the door with a regretful look washed across her face. I guess she must have been worried about what I would do to her husband, and it was wise for one to get to know a bitch before you start running your mouth off to her. Apparently she hadn't done her homework to know what I was capable of doing.

I hurried to put on some clothes, then made my way to the address Marva had written on the paper. When I got to Christina's house, which looked like a tiny shack, I couldn't believe that Desmon's car was parked in the driveway. I was seriously going through the emotions right now, and I didn't know why I was so upset with Desmon, especially when he wasn't even my husband. But then I thought about the lies. I thought about the promises. Even thought about the way he fucked me, and told me over and over again how the two of us would eventually be together.

There weren't too many niggas who I gave myself to, and whenever I did give up the pussy, I always gave it to niggas who I thought were worthy of me. I knew that confronting Desmon about this shit would end my career, and I would never be able to show my face at work again.

For a few minutes, I sat in the car, gazing at the gun that sat on my lap. My legs trembled as I contemplated what to do, and there was no doubt that I wanted this nigga to feel the hurt he had caused me.

I was so mad that I couldn't even cry. Mama always said that crying over a nigga was never worth a drop, and that tears were for weak bitches who had lost power. Right now, I felt powerless. I felt used and disgusted with myself for trusting that this nigga would do right by me. Married or not, I believed him when he said he didn't love his wife. I believed when he said it was all about me, and the amount of time that we spent together was ridiculous. I didn't know how he was able to pull this shit off, but he successfully did so, because there was another bitch out there like me who didn't give a fuck that he was married.

Christina didn't care, and I assumed that she had been suckered into this just like I had been. She and Desmon had probably been at this for quite some time, and according to her, she had been with the company for the past ten years. There was no telling how long this bullshit had been going on, but no matter how long, I needed some answers.

I opened the car door and slowly walked to the front door with a hoody and some jeans on. My phone had the nerve to ring, and seeing that it was Mama calling, I let the call go to voice mail. When she called back, I put my cell phone on silent. It alarmed me that she was calling at this time, but I figured that she wanted to discuss what had happened earlier. Right now, I wasn't in the mood to go there with her.

From the outside, the inside of the house looked dark, but as I peeked in the inside, I could see a sliver of light in one of the rooms. Attempting to get inside, I slid my credit card between the door crack and the lock. I wiggled the card around and kept turning the knob until the wooden door came open. It squeaked, but the sound of the door was drowned out by hip-hop music. The fact that Christina was listening to hip-hop music was a shock to me, but I guess her whole demeanor had been a front.

I quietly closed the door and tiptoed down the carpeted hallway. Obviously, all Desmon was doing for this bitch was giving her some good dick, because the whole damn house looked crappy and outdated. The furniture looked like shit from the 80's, and the pictures she had hanging crooked on the walls looked like they came from the Goodwill. The way she dressed implied that too, but that shit didn't matter to Desmon. He was in it to win it, and I could tell by the moans and groans I heard coming from the bathroom. The door was cracked and I could hear the shower running. Loud grunts and the sound of bodies slapping together could be heard too. I didn't want to be seen just yet, so I peeked around the door until I saw the wet glass shower that was filled with steam. Christina straddled Desmon, but her flat ass was pressed against the glass shower door. He pounded against her so hard that I thought he was going to break that shaky glass. Her panties were lying on the floor, and so was the Nike outfit that he'd had on earlier.

"Ooooh, shit this hurts," Christina hollered out with each hard thrust that Desmon pumped into her. "Bu . . . but this big dick of yours feels so good to me, baby. You got this pussy talking to you, don't you?"

Desmon was like a raging bull. The grip he had on Christina's ass had turned it red. His grunts got louder and louder, especially when he pulled out of her and shoved his dick into her mouth. As swift as he was pumping, I was sure he was going to knock out some of that heifer's crooked teeth. His hands were wrapped tightly around her dirty blonde hair, while she sucked his dick like a professional porn star.

"Sssss . . . suck it, bitch," Desmon directed. "Go deep and kill it!"

Christina's head was moving so fast. Watching her almost gave me a damn headache. Their sex session was nothing like ours. Desmon was always calm, gentle, and careful with his words. It was as if I was watching a different man, one that had me in total shock as I continued to watch him getting it in with Christina. She backed away from his dick and dropped to her knees as he faced the wall. When she started licking his asshole, and I heard him screaming out like a bitch, that was when I had had enough. I lifted the gun in my hand and fired one shot into the glass door, intentionally missing them both. The glass shattered everywhere, and I couldn't believe when I saw Desmon reach for Christina and use her as a shield.

"The fuck?" he shouted and trembled with her in front of him. She trembled too, and tears began to rush down her snow white face. Both of their eyes were bugged as they stared at me in fear.

"Do . . . please don't hurt us," Christina cried out. "I . . . I didn't want to do any of this, I swear. Desmon made me do it."

I couldn't help but to laugh. "That's right, bitch. Throw that nigga under the bus to save your own ass. I don't blame you, not one bit. After all, somebody must pay for my pain and sufferin', and for my wasted time."

I used my cell phone to take a few pictures of them, and at that moment I realized that Desmon was worth more to me alive than he was dead.

"Baby, let me talk to you," he said, trying to sweet talk me. "Thi . . . this has all been one big mistake. This bitch don't mean anything to me, and the only reason I'm here is because I thought you were upset with me about what happened earlier. Marva was sweating me, and when I called you didn't answer your phone. Give me a minute to put on my clothes. Then we can get out of here and go somewhere private. I'm so sorry about this, and the last thing I ever wanted to do was hurt you, sweetheart. I'm telling you right now that I don't give a damn about anyone but you."

It was so funny that I could now see through his bullshit lies. It took all of this for me to see who I was really dealing with, and it was such an ugly thing.

I waved the gun around and told Christina to leave. "Now, bitch. Before I change my mind and blow yo' damn brains out."

She rushed out of the shower and slipped on the wet floor as she ran past me with cuts on her feet from the glass. I wanted to knock the shit out of her, but my beef was with Desmon. I inched my way up to the shower and held the gun up to his face. His scary-ass crouched down, and as I looked at him, I couldn't help but to think about the times Mama spoke about these pretty, money making niggas who were cowards. They definitely knew how to make money, but they damn sure didn't have any guts.

"I came here for an explanation, but you know what, nigga? This is all the answers I need. You can get back to fuckin' your dirty whore after I leave, but in the meantime, I'll be contactin' you tomorrow with my bank account number. I'm not sure how much money I'll be demandin' just yet, but be sure to have plenty of it ready, especially if you don't want anyone to see these pictures. That includes your wife, who may be able to use them against you in court. So think real hard about how you want to handle this. With that, I'm out. Don't bother to call me again, but I will most definitely be callin' you."

I started to walk away, but I had to get one fucking crack against his face with the gun. I caught him off guard and slammed the gun against his face as hard as I could. Unfortunately, though, I was so mad that I didn't stop there. As he crouched down and shielded his face, I pistol whipped his ass until I got tired. The blows from the gun tore at his skin, causing plenty of wounds that started to bleed.

"Tha . . . that's enough," he shouted and flopped to the floor of the shower with blood and water dripping down the side of his face. His lip was busted, and redness could be seen in his right eye where I'd hit him. When he opened his mouth, I saw his front tooth dangling, trying to hang on.

"Go," he said in a whisper while gazing at me behind his watery eyes. "I . . . I'm sorry, and I'll have your money ready to . . . tomorrow."

"Good. And I'm sorry too."

I uppercut his ass with the butt of the gun, trying to break his fucking jaw. Wasn't sure if I accomplished that or not, but his head slumped and he covered his face with his hands. I backed away from that piece of shit, and as I made my way to the front door, I saw Christina sitting on the couch sobbing.

"Ple . . . please don't tell anyone about this," she cried. "I don't want to lose my job, and I don't want anyone to see those pictures. I wish that none of this ever happened."

"Me either, Christina. But unfortunately, it did. And you know what? I wouldn't want no one to see you sucking a black man's asshole either. Allow me to spare you the embarrassment."

From just a few feet away, I lifted the gun and squeezed the trigger. The bullet whistled through the air and landed in the middle of her forehead. She fell back on the couch and her eyes stayed wide open as she stared at the squeaking ceiling fan from above. I honestly do not know why I wanted to kill the bitch, but I was in a trigger happy mood and couldn't control it. Christina couldn't benefit me in anyway. Desmon could, so his ass was lucky to be alive. I wasn't sure how I was going to spin this madness, and by the time I reached my car I was a nervous fucking wreck. I sped off, but my hands were shaking so badly that I pulled my car over about three blocks away and parked. I reached for my phone, and in a serious panic I called Mama.

"Don't do it," she said as if she were wide awake. "I mean it, Chyna, don't do it."

"Do what?"

"Don't you do anything to Desmon or to anyone who is involved with him. I suspect that his wife stopped by to see you. All she wants is for you to do the dirty work for her, and you'll be a damn fool for killing Desmon like she wants you to do."

"Ho . . . how do you know his wife came by to see me?"

"How many times do I have to tell y'all that when y'all think I'm not paying attention, I am? Because of what happened today, I had somebody watching you. I wanted to make sure that Desmon's wife didn't try anything stupid, and last I heard was that she was at your apartment. I also heard that you left, and when Marva was stopped by the person I asked to go there, she told them that you were on your way to see Desmon at another bitch's house. I kept calling you because I didn't want you to do anything stupid. Let that nigga be, Chyna, and I hope like hell that you didn't do anything that you're going to regret."

I sat silent for a while and stared ahead in thought. A slow tear dripped down my face as I thought about what I had already done. "It's too late," I said in a tearful voice. "It's too late, Mama, and I'm so sick and tired of bein' fucked over by these niggas. Why do they keep on doin' this shit, and why can't I find a nigga who want to be real with me and do right? Is it that goddamn hard for a nigga to treat a bitch right?"

"Maybe, maybe not, but you've made some bad choices, Chyna. This shit is on you, and you've got to stop running around here like some sick, dick-whipped trick who don't know any better. At the end of the day, that nigga was married and you didn't have no business with him. Whether he was having problems with his wife or not, his ass was off limits, and you should have focused your time and energy elsewhere. He promised you the world, and for whatever reason, you thought that fool could deliver. What is wrong with you for believing that dumb shit, and have I not taught you better?"

"You did, but I hate it when you're so right. I hate that I keep getting this love shit wrong, and all I want to do is experience real love with somebody who can keep it one hundred with me. Is there something wrong with that? Am I asking for too damn much?"

I slammed my hand on the steering wheel and slumped down in the seat. I began to sob like a baby, and that was the last thing that Mama wanted to hear.

"Chyna, pull yourself together! You need to—"

"I can't," I cried out and hit the steering wheel again. "This shit hurts, Mama! It hurts, and for one damn time in my life I just need to let this shit out and cry about it! I'm tired . . . so tired of feelin' fuckin' used by niggas! Don't you understand this pain . . . do you even know what this shit feels like?"

"Hell yes, I do! And I've done all that I could do to school you and your sisters about the love game and hip y'all to how some niggas get down. My goddamn motto is, don't know love or show love, unless it's for the love of family. I say that shit because there are so many cut-throat niggas who don't deserve yo' love. When you open yourself up to those fools, this is what happens. The good thing is, wounds heal. But the scars remain. Feel those scars and revisit them every time a nigga step to you and try to spill that foolishness that Desmon swung your way. Next time, be ready for it, Chyna, and stop playing the fool. Chalk this shit up as a loss, and don't let the bullshit happen to you again."

I swallowed the lump in my throat and rubbed my aching forehead. "I'll try, but in the meantime, what am I goin' to do about this situation?"

"What do you mean? What about your situation? Did you do something to Desmon?"

"I pistol whipped his ass and wanted to kill him but I didn't. I did, however, have to deal with his trick because she kept mouthing off to me and I didn't appreciate that shit."

I could hear Mama release a deep breath. She remained silent.

"I know what you're thinkin'," I said. "But I worked with that white bitch on my job, and I felt betrayed by her, too. The only reason I didn't do anything to Desmon—"

"Wait one goddamn minute," Mama interrupted. "Did you say white bitch? Are you telling me that you went up into a white bitch's house and put her ass to sleep?"

"If that's how you want to put it, yes."

"Chyna, where are you? How far away are you from that trick's house?"

"A few blocks away. Why?"

"Bitch, you listen to me and listen to me good. Get yo' ass away from there right now. Hurry to this hotel and be ready to take yo' ass back to Cali with me in a few hours."

"Why? Why are you trippin' out? I already have an idea about how I'm goin' to spin this, and as soon as Desmon up the money—"

"Didn't I tell you what would happen if you ever killed a white bitch? You know how the police are when it comes to them, and I always told you to only go there if it were a life-threatening situation. Please tell me that was the case, because I have a bad feeling about this shit. Yo' ass is going to need one hell of a defense."

I sat up straight when I heard sirens from a distance. Maybe Mama was right, and it was time for me to get the fuck out of there. I pulled my car away from the curb, and could still hear the sounds of police sirens. "Mama, what hotel are you at again?"

"I'm at the Four Seasons on East Delaware Place. If you don't think you can make it here, hurry to Honey's place and I'll come get you from there."

The urgency in Mama's voice, along with the loud sirens, made me panic. I was speeding so fast that I didn't notice a police car coming my way. I slowed down, but the car made a U-turn and headed my way. "A police car is followin' me," I shouted to Mama. "What should I do? Should I try to out run him?"

"Damn, Chyna! I can't believe this shit! I ha . . . hate to say this to you, but put that muthafuckin' pedal to the floor and after you lose him, jump out of that damn car and run! Do it now, focus, hang up this phone, and I expect a call from you real soon!"

I looked at the flashing lights in my rearview mirror and smacked away my flowing tears. "In a minute, Mama. I love you."

"I love you too. Now go!"

My foot hit the accelerator and I burned hella rubber as I sped off down the street, trying to get away from the police car. I was moving so fast that my car was shaking and the speedometer needle could go no further. At this time in the morning, I was lucky that the streets were clear. I was able to dash down the streets, and when I made it to the highway, I swerved in and out of the minimal traffic to get away from the police.

My heart was racing and my palms were sweating so much that my hands could barely stay gripped on the steering wheel. My eyes were blurred from the falling tears, and my head was banging from my deep thoughts. I seriously thought I could get away with this, but by the time I reached three more exits, several more police vehicles had joined in on the chase. I made a sharp turn off the highway that made my car feel as though it was on two wheels. The bumps in the road caused my body to jump and when there was not one police car in sight, I slammed on the brakes and jumped out of the car. Not knowing where I was, I ran down a grassy hill and attempted to hide myself in a close by wooded area with a bunch of trees. My phone was in my pocket and it kept on ringing. I knew it was Mama calling me, but as I reached into my pocket, that was when I saw the helicopter's bright lights. The lights were so bright that they lit up the entire area like Christmas tree. I hurried to call Mama, and the only thing that I was able to say to her was . . . "They got me."

"Drop the gun or we'll shoot!" The officers yelled.

I dropped the phone, causing it to crash as it hit the ground. I then raised my hands in the air and yelled loudly so they could hear me. "It's a phone! Not a gun! Please don't shoot!"

Several officers moved in on me, and they hurried to drop me to the ground. As the cuffs were put on me, I couldn't help but think about one person—Mama.

# *Karrine*

## 10

Mama woke me out of my sleep, cussing and fussing about what was going on with Chyna. She explained everything to me, and all I could do was drop back on the sofa in the hotel room and cry. My heart ached, because I definitely didn't want my sister to go out like this. There was no way in hell that she was in police custody, and I was so sure that Mama would come up with a plan or something to get Chyna out of this shit.

Mama slammed the phone down, almost breaking it. "Where in the fuck is Honey?" she shouted. "I've been trying to reach that nigga for hours and he hasn't returned any of my goddamn phone calls!"

Hearing her say that made me cry harder. When Honey left his house earlier, he seemed to be on a mission. One that I could in no way stop, so there was no telling where he was. I told Mama about the suspicious car from earlier, and I also told her about the phone call he'd gotten.

"So you don't have no idea who he was talking to?" she asked.

"No. For all I knew, I thought he was talkin' to you. All . . . all of this craziness needs to stop. What do you think is goin' to happen to Chyna?"

Mama was puffing on her cigarette like it was going out of style. I had never seen her this frantic before, and all she kept doing was pacing the floor with her cell phone in her hand. She patted the cell phone against her leg while in deep thought.

"Call Simone," she said to me. "Tell her to come here right now."

I used my cell phone to call Simone. It was almost five o'clock in the morning, and when she answered she sounded as if she were still asleep.

"Chyna's been arrested," I said. "Mama wants you to come to the hotel right now."

"Arrested? For what?"

"I'll tell you about it when you get here. Just come, okay?"

Simone said that she was on her way. I looked at Mama, who kept taking deep breaths, trying to calm herself. I seriously thought she was going to have a heart attack, and when I told her to sit down and chill, she halted her steps and glared at me.

"Chill? How in the fuck do you expect for me to chill when my goddamn daughter may be charged with murder? I can't find that lousy-ass nigga, Honey, and if you want to do something, why don't you call some of that bastard's hoes to find out where the fuck he is."

Mama was out of line, but I kept my mouth shut and didn't say shit. The last thing she needed right now was to pick a fight with me, because I was already on edge about her and this drug selling bullshit with Honey anyway. I was worried about him, too, and for Shania's sake, I truly hoped that everything was okay.

Mama's cell phone rang, causing my heart to drop somewhere below my stomach. I was relieved when I heard her say Honey's name.

"I've been calling you for hours!" Mama shouted. "Please get over here so you can help me deal with this shit with Chyna. She's been arrested, and I am losing my goddamn mind trying to figure out what to do!"

Mama didn't wait for a reply. She threw the phone at the wall, breaking the phone into pieces.

I stood and walked up to Mama, holding her shoulders so she could face me. "Mama, please," I begged. "Please calm down and stop actin' like this. I know you're worried, but Chyna won't be able to call if you're around here breakin' phones. We will all get through this, and it may not be as bad as we think."

Mama stared at me with so much anger and hurt trapped in her eyes. For as long as I could remember, I never, ever saw my mother cry. Tears filled her eyes and she did her best to fight back tears that were trying to escape. She opened her mouth, but no words came out. She swallowed, but the lump in her throat wouldn't go away. She then touched her chest and squeezed it. "That's my baby," Mama said. "Wha . . . what am I going to do if they lock up my child and keep her behind bars forever, Karrine? You already know that if she is charged with murdering a white bitch, you . . . you know what they're going to do to her. She will rot in jail until the day she dies."

Mama dropped her head, and I couldn't believe that she was crying on my shoulder. I tried to be the strong one here, but seeing her like this hurt me so bad. It hurt me because after all of this time, I finally witnessed how deep Mama's love for us really was. She never wanted to see any of us hurt, and she tried to prevent all that she could by displaying tough love.

I embraced Mama and we cried together. It was a mother and daughter moment that I was sure the two of us would never forget. It was a moment that neither of us wanted to let go of.

"This is too much on you, Mama. Free us, and whatever happens . . . it just happens. We will all fight to the end for Chyna, and whatever you need for me to do, I will do it. But once this is over, let us go. That includes Honey—you've got to free him from your stronghold too. He's goin' to get killed if you don't, and we just can't keep travelin' down this path, expectin' that none of us will have to suffer the consequences from the way we're livin'."

Mama backed away from me and wiped her tears. "I did set y'all free, Karrine, but every time I look up y'all keep running back to me. You're a prime example, so how am I supposed to move on when y'all keep putting me in the middle of y'all's mess? I don't want to turn my back, and the first person that y'all call when there is trouble is me. It's been hard for me not to be there for y'all, and I've never been the kind of mother who can just completely walk away from my children for good."

"I know, but at this point you've done all that you can do. We've got to live with the choices we've made, and so be it. I guess you're goin' to have to finally kick me the hell out of your crib and trust me to be the best mother that I can be to Shania. You're goin' to have to hold Chyna's hand through this process, but let go whenever the final judgment is made. Simone seems like the only one who may not depend on you as much, and as for Honey, he is not with it Mama. His loyalty to you supersedes everything else, but he is one unhappy man. I know how you feel about the business aspect of things, but you need to release him. If you don't want to let go of the business, put somebody else in charge that you trust. You trust Trice, so why don't you let her run things? Maybe even run things yourself. Honey has had enough, and he may not tell you this, but I know that he wants out."

Our mother-daughter moment was over. Mama walked away from me and stood by the window, looking out. "Karrine, you always think you have the right answers to everything. But the truth is, you don't. Honey already knows that there is no out in this business. You just can't pack it up one day and walk away. I've spent years and years building this empire. This is what I do, and the only person who I trust to handle shit for me is Honey. So any little fantasies that you have about him and you being husband and wife, living in a house with a white picket fence, kids running around and him working a nine-to-five job . . . sweetheart, you can forget that shit. It ain't happening, and Honey will tell you that himself. He may spill some bullshit to you from time to time, but when all is said and done, that nigga will always choose work over pussy and pleasure."

"Maybe so. But I wonder if it ever really came down to it, if he would one day choose love."

Mama turned around and chuckled. "Love? Really? So called "love" is why Chyna is in the predicament that she's in today. Love beat yo' ass several months ago and had you running to me for help. Love has cheated on you time and time again, and love was just at one of his many hoes' houses with his dick in her mouth. That's why love didn't answer his phone. So my suggestion to you, Karrine, is for you to put your big-girl panties on and wake the fuck up. Save the love talk for another day, because today is surely not the day for a confession."

I had to swallow hard from her harsh words of reality, but I still defended what I said. "You're right, Mama, but love can make people change. It can make a person want to do the right things, especially when they recognize that the path they're on is reckless. Now, I don't want to talk about this anymore. What's gon' be will be. Right now we need to concern ourselves with Chyna and figure out what we need to do to help her through this unfortunate situation."

Thank God Mama was willing to change the subject. This battle between she, Honey, and I couldn't be won, and it was up to him to tell her exactly how he felt. I tried to break it down to Mama, but she was convinced that Honey was never going anywhere.

Almost an hour later, Simone showed up, and so did Honey. Mama told them everything that had happened, and we all agreed that it did not look good for Chyna. We waited for her phone call, and when she called my phone, she asked to speak to Mama.

"Honey and me will be there soon," Mama said. "Whatever happens, you'll be represented by the best, and I will do everything within my power to make sure you don't remain in jail."

We all had a lot of faith in Mama, but I wasn't so sure about this. A murder charge was nothing to play with, and I had a feeling that all the money in the world wouldn't be able to save Chyna from the craziness she'd gotten herself into over a married man.

All I knew was that this was a bad-ass feeling. It made me think about all that I had been doing, and how easy it was for me to squeeze the trigger when shit didn't go down like I wanted it to. Lord knows I'd done my dirt, and I guess I was being a fool if I believed there would never be any consequences.

Simone had left the room with Shania, and Mama and Honey were getting ready to go. We hadn't said much to each other, but right after Mama walked out, I called Honey's name. He turned at the door.

"We're driving in my car," he said to Mama. "I'll be there in a minute."

"Hurry up," she said. "I want to get this taken care of, Honey."

He closed the door and stood with his arms crossed. "What's up?"

"So, how did it go? Did you find out who was in that car?"

"Yep."

"And?"

His face twisted and his tone went up a notch. "And what, Karrine? You already know what went down, so I don't get why you're asking."

"I'm askin' because I care. When and where does it end, Honey? When does this shit stop? Do you want to die? Your life is on the line every single day, and the more niggas that you kill, the more enemies you're creatin'."

He sighed. "Are you done? I must say that I'm getting real tired of you burning all this fucking bread on me. Do you ever have something positive to say? The bottom line is, I did what I had to do. If I didn't get those niggas, they were coming for me. Did you expect for me to sit back and wait for them to get at me?"

It was so apparent that I kept running into a brick wall with this. Honey and Mama were driving me crazy, and I didn't understand why it was so hard for me to let this shit go.

"I guess not, Honey. Just go and see about Chyna. If you get a chance, talk to Mama too. I already spoke to her a little about how you've been feelin', but maybe she'll listen to you, because she wasn't tryin' to hear anything from me."

"You can't talk to Mama about how I really feel, because you don't know how I really feel. Stay out of my fuckin' business, Karrine, and stop sweatin' me about so much shit! This ain't going down like you want it to, and when you get done talkin', my loyalty will remain with one person and one person only. You already know who she is, and she's waitin' for me in the car."

On that note, Honey walked out. And today was the day that I washed my hands of it all. When Simone came back, I left the hotel a few hours later, and Shania and I went to Chyna's place for the night. I prayed on her situation and prayed for myself, too. I had no idea what tomorrow would bring, but whatever went down, I vowed to limit my relationship with Mama, as well as with Honey.

# *HONEY*

## 11

For the last several months, shit had been real hectic. Mama had been tripping out because of the situation with Chyna, and the best that our lawyers could do was cop a plea deal that smacked her with ten years instead of twenty-five to life. Chyna claimed it was self-defense, and after I had a "talk" with Desmon, he also confessed that Chyna had killed Christina because she attacked Chyna. His admission still wasn't enough for the charges to be dropped, so Chyna had to do the time and be done with it.

Watching our family go through this bullshit had my thoughts all over the place. I thought about if it were me on lockdown, instead of Chyna. I had been doing shit that I didn't have the guts to tell Mama that I was doing, and there was a time when I would seek her approval before putting a nigga to sleep. But things had changed. I had so much money and power that I started to feel invincible. I was very arrogant, and at the snap of my finger, bitches would fall to their knees begging for some attention. My head had swelled. I was high off life, but my heart was motherfucking broken—shattered into a thousand and one pieces, because Karrine had vacated the premises in my life and was barely speaking to me.

All I know was she had moved out of Mama's house in Cali and came back to Chicago. She and Mama had a big argument over where Shania would live, and Mama was fucked up in the head because Shania wasn't with her anymore. The shit messed me up too, and every time I called Karrine about seeing my daughter, she wouldn't answer the phone. She never told me where she lived, and I had to get one of my boys on it to find out where in the fuck she was. He gave me her address, and I went to her crib that day and clowned on her. I threatened to take her to court, just so I could have some kind of time with my daughter. I hated that she was trying to keep Shania from me, and I knew exactly why Mama was so upset about the situation, too. It was wrong on so many different levels, but when I broke that shit down to her, Karrine agreed to Shania staying with me every other weekend.

I was on my way to Karrine's crib to pick up Shania. My family, on Ray's side of the family, was having a reunion at the park. I asked Mama if she wanted to go, but she cussed me the hell out for asking. I saw it as an opportunity for her to spend some time with Shania, but she didn't see it that way. She had so much animosity against Ray's side of the family, so maybe it was a good thing that she rejected my offer. I didn't ask Karrine because I already knew what her answer would be. So it was all about me and my baby girl today, and I was pleased about that.

With hanging cargo shorts, a wife-beater, and clean white tennis shoes on, I stood on Karrine's porch and rang the doorbell. The ranch-style crib she lived in was just enough for her and Shania, but it was nothing compared to what she was used to living in. I was surprised that she'd chosen this place, but she had probably chosen it because it was almost an hour away from where I lived.

Karrine opened the door looking sexy as fuck in a purple tank shirt with thin straps. Her tiny nipples left imprints in the shirt, and the stretch shorts she wore melted on the curves of her hips and ass. My heart raced every time I saw her, but like always, our conversation was short. Shania was on Karrine's hip, and she handed her over to me right at the door.

"Let me go get her overnight bag," Karrine said. "I'll bring it out to the car."

She walked away, and I gazed at her ass cheeks that the shorts weren't big enough to hide. Trying to get my mind out of the gutter, I kissed my baby girl on the cheek and carried her to the car. As I was securing her in the car seat, she was all smiles and was playing with a Barbie doll. Karrine had Shania dressed in a colorful sundress that matched her sandals. White framed sunglasses covered her eyes, and her long hair was combed into a sleek ponytail held by colorful ribbons.

"Girl, I'ma have to keep my eyes on you," I said to Shania. "You gon' be a heartbreaker like yo' mama."

"You mean like her daddy," Karrine said as she walked up to the car. I moved aside as she put the overnight bag into the car and bent over to give her good-byes to Shania.

"Have fun today, and I'll see you tomorrow. Be good, and I want another big ole kiss before you go, okay?"

Shania nodded and kissed Karrine. She also made her Barbie doll kiss Karrine too, and they both laughed.

As Karrine was bent over, I stroked the minimal hair on my chin and studied her ass. It had been a long time since we had fucked, and my hard dick was stretching the shit out of my shorts, trying to get at her. I didn't want her to know how eager I was to feel the warmness of her pussy again, so I didn't make a move. But when she leaned further into the car to move Shania's bag to the other side, I stood behind her. I wanted her to feel my growing muscle, but she hurried to back out of the car.

"Let me help you with that," I said, trying to play it off.

"I got it. Now, move back and please don't get that close to me."

I backed away with my hands in the air. "Damn. Sorry. I was only trying to help."

"Sure," she said, then waved good-bye to Shania.

She didn't say anything else to me. Just walked away and headed inside. I continued to stare at her ass, and it was one beautiful sight. It was as if Karrine was purposely swaying her hips from side to side, just to give me a fucking heart attack.

"I see you, ma. But it's okay. Play a nigga all you want to . . . I'm good."

She didn't bother to turn around. All she did was go inside and close the door. I got in the car, but on the drive to the park I couldn't shake Karrine from my thoughts. I paid no attention to the ringing of my cell phone, which was probably one of those bitches who could never steal my heart from Karrine. I don't know why I kept depriving myself of her, but then again, I knew. She wanted me to choose. I did, and since my decision had been made, I had to fight my feelings for her and deal with it.

My baby girl and I kicked it at the park with family. My uncle, Ned, was barbecuing, my Aunt Betty was clowning on people with jokes, and plenty of my relatives sat on benches getting their grub on. Some were playing volleyball, while others were dancing to the loud music that was booming through two big speakers. Shania was moving from one person to the next. My aunts and cousins were all over her, and everybody wanted to hold her.

"She is so damn pretty," my cousin Anna said while holding Shania. "Nigga how did you pull this shit off?"

"That's what I'm sayin'," one of my cousins from Mississippi said. "I mean, yo' ass fine as fuck, but that chile must'a got mama's genes."

"She look just like Honey to me," another aunt said in my defense. "He spit her out, so I don't know what the hell y'all talking about."

"Thank you," I said to my aunt. "Shania looks more like me than she does Karrine."

I had a picture of Karrine in my wallet, so I pulled out her picture to show it to my peeps. Some said Shania looked like me, while others said Karrine.

"I don't give a shit who she looks like," my cousin Ricky said. "She's adorable and her daddy is loaded with cash. Nigga, why don't you lay a little somethin' on me? At least a grand, so I can get this car I've been havin' my eyes on."

As Ricky held out his hand, all I did was slap it with mine. My family knew what time it was, and I wasn't giving nobody shit, unless they worked with, or for me.

My cousin's thirteen-year-old daughter, Tracy, ran off with Shania on her hip. Tracy took Shania over to her other cousins, and they began to blow big bubbles in the air and try to pop them. Shania was having herself a good time and so was I. I sat down to play cards, drink whiskey, and get high as fuck with several of my uncles and cousins. The game kept getting delayed by the ongoing conversation about finances, jobs, and pussy. Everybody was broke, nobody liked their jobs, and the bitches on their teams weren't worth two cents.

"Sounds like you niggas need to take a new path and try door number two," I advised. "It couldn't be that bad, is it?"

"Nah, it ain't that bad," my cousin Jake from St. Louis said. "Niggas just makin' bad choices. I'ma try door number three, in hopes that when I open it there is a wad of cash waitin' for me, a good payin' job, and two or three more bitches to add to my collection."

I shrugged, some laughed, and some added their wishes for what was behind door number three. My cousin, Ruby, brought each of us plates piled with barbecue. As I got ready to get my grub on, I looked around for Shania. She was still running around with Tracy and her other cousins. I watched from a short distance as my baby girl fell a few times but got right back up. She turned in her pretty dress, and kept picking up a huge ball, trying to throw it high in the air. After that, I saw her dancing to the music. I wanted to get up and dance with her, but my head was spinning from drinking so much, and I felt kind of woozy.

"Muthafucka, play what's in yo' hand and stop lookin' at what's in mine," Jake yelled at another one of my cousins.

"I don't give a fuck what's in yo' hand, nigga. This game belongs to me."

Those niggas started arguing over a stupid game, and I couldn't believe how serious the argument had gotten. It was obvious that they were beefing about something else, and when Jake started cussing about the money that my other cousin owed him, the argument made sense.

We all had to sober up and break them apart from each other. But as we were trying to calm the confusion between them, the sound of a bunch of firecrackers popping rang out in my ears. My vision was slightly blurred from being so high, and the smoke from the barbecue made it hard to see what was going on. It didn't take me long to figure out that the firecracker sound was actually gunfire. Everybody was running, people were dropping to the ground, and several of my relatives were firing shots at two cars that rolled on the set, spraying bullets. The cries of children rang out in my ears, screams could be heard miles away, and the ongoing sound of gunfire made me dizzy. I could see my baby girl on the ground, right next to Tracy, who was holding Shania in her arms. I felt like I was running in slow motion as I rushed over to them, and as they were clearly in my sight, I could immediately see that several of the bullets had hit Tracy in the head. Blood covered her and Shania, but as Shania lay there crying I snatched her up and touched all over her body with my trembling hands. From all of the blood that was on her, I was so sure that she had been hit, but it appeared that all she had was a scarred face from falling and bloody knees.

I quickly turned my attention to Tracy and dropped to my knees next to her. Chaos, shock, and complete pandemonium were all around me, and I felt as if I were in a dream, wanting to get out. But this was no dream. I held Tracy's lifeless, bloody body in my arms, and looked around at several of my other relatives who lay dead. The screams and cries echoed throughout the park, and sirens could be heard from a distance. I continued to hold Tracy in my arms while Shania clung to me and cried.

"Traaaaacyyyyyy!" I heard her mother scream. "Oh God, no, pleeeeease!"

She dropped to her knees next to me and reached for her dead child. After she screamed again, I was so out of it that I didn't know what the fuck was going on. All I remembered doing was picking up Shania and holding her tight as she wrapped her arms around my neck. After that, I walked away in a daze.

The crime scene was nothing pretty. At least twenty police cars were on the set, several ambulances, and news reporters. I called Karrine about twenty minutes ago, telling her to come to the park to get Shania. I couldn't get into details about what had happened because there was so much going on. The police had arrested several of my family members who had warrants, many bodies were covered with white sheets, and everybody was trying to find out who the fuck had done this.

At first, I wasn't even sure if this shit was on me, but the word got around quickly that it may have been some niggas who were after my cousin Vinney.

Whoever had done it, they would be dealt with right away. This was uncalled for, and even though I considered myself to be one cold-ass nigga at times, never would I do any goddamn thing like this.

"Jake, Stan, and Poncho hopped in his car and jetted," my uncle whispered to me as I leaned against my car, gazing at the scene. "They went after those niggas and got two of them already. We gots to find out who those other niggas were, and as soon as the police get done here, we gon' rock the fuck out of Chicago tonight."

I nodded and kissed Shania's forehead as she rested her head against my chest. She had fallen asleep, and I couldn't help, but to think how fucking lucky I was right now.

As I was in thought, I saw Karrine walking my way. Her eyes were widened as she looked around at the scene, and she rushed up to me with tears in her eyes. The dried blood all over Shania's dress, the scar on her face, and her scraped knees made Karrine frown. She snatched Shania from my arms and held her close to her chest.

"Wha . . . what in the hell happened?" she shouted.

I didn't appreciate her tone, but I remained calm. "Some niggas got real bold and thought it was a good idea to spray the scene."

Karrine pulled Shania away from her chest to look at her face. "Honey, noooo," she said tearfully. "Please don't tell me that you allowed this to happen. Don't tell me this happened because you—"

"Let me stop you right there. We don't know why this happened, but we're in the process of trying to find out. Now take Shania home, and I'll call you later with more info."

Karrine lost it. Her face twisted and she spoke through gritted teeth. "Don't bother to call me ever! This is the main reason why I didn't want Shania to be with yo' ass; I knew some bullshit like this was goin' to happen! I knew it, Honey, so you can do whatever you gotta do in a court of fuckin' law. I'm goin' to fight for what's mine, and I'll be damned if Shania is ever allowed to go anywhere with yo' crooked-ass again!"

My uncle stepped back as if he was in shock by Karrine's harsh words. People were looking at us, and even the police were starting to walk our way.

"Ten. Nine. Eight. Seven—and just to warn you," I said. "When I get to one, if you're still standing in front of me talkin' that bullshit, I'm going to jail for kickin' yo' muthafuckin' ass! I said we'll talk later, and I won't repeat myself again."

Karrine moved forward and stood face to face with me. "Nigga, do what you gotta do. I won't repeat myself either, and I meant what the fuck I said. You can take that phone call you mentioned and shove it up yo' ass. I'm done tryin' to be nice to you, and you'd better be thankin' yo' lucky stars that my muthafuckin' baby girl is still alive!"

I tightened my fists, wanting so badly to crack this bitch dead in her face. It took everything I had not to beat her ass for acting a damn fool at a time like this, but I held back. I bit into my lip and stared into her eyes with much anger trapped in mine. Karrine wanted to get a reaction from me, but that didn't happen.

"Yeah, that's what I thought," she said, continuing to push me.

I felt like a punk.

"Good riddance, nigga, and take one last look at yo' daughter 'cause you'll never be able to see her again."

Karrine rolled her eyes and stormed off. I was so mad that I slammed my fist on the hood of my car, causing a huge dent in it. Thing is, I didn't know if I was mad at Karrine or mad at myself for putting my daughter in a situation like this one. At the family reunion or not, there was still a possibility that those niggas were after me.

***

Slowly but surely, things were going downhill. For the next several weeks, eleven of my family members had been put to rest. I paid for every single funeral and attended all of them as well. I was drained, disgusted, and frustrated as fuck. Frustrated because I didn't have nobody to talk to about all the shit I was feeling. Mama didn't want to hear about it, and I didn't want to come off like a whiny bitch and talk to my boys. Like I had said before, Mama hated Ray's side of the family and she didn't give a fuck about none of them. Therefore, talking this shit out with her was out. I hadn't bothered to call Karrine, and from the way things were going, it was probably a good thing that Shania was with her instead of with me.

This go around, what had happened at the family reunion, wasn't on me. The niggas who shot up the picnic were there to settle a beef with two of my cousins who had robbed them five days before. No matter what, though, the shit was wrong. Innocent people were killed, so we all had to get down to business the other night. It was a blood bath in Chicago, and many of the news channels had covered the ongoing murders that transpired across the city. By now, I had done so much shit that I was starting to get paranoid. I watched the cameras in my house like a hawk, and I didn't even go take a shit without my Glock by my side. I figured this feeling wouldn't last for long, but there I was, weeks after, still feeling the same way.

"I don't know what else to tell you," Mama said as I sat in my bed, listening to her over the phone. "But I do know that I need you at one hundred percent next month when we close on that deal I've been talking to you about for months. I'm counting on you, Honey, and this is going to be a huge payday for us. So, take two aspirins, call me in the morning, and let me know how you're feeling."

I hit the END button to disconnect the call, and I lifted my head when I saw Candice come into my bedroom carrying a tray in her hand. All she wore were some nude lace boyshorts. Her chocolate, perky breasts looked like round melons, and I was known for only sticking my dick in pretty bitches. She had been here since last night, but I still hadn't fucked her. I hadn't been in the mood, and there was too much shit on my mind that didn't involve pussy.

"Happy Birthday to you; happy birthday to you . . ." Candice sang as she carried the tray up to my bed. On top of the tray was breakfast, along with a cupcake and a candle stuck in it. "Now, make a wish and blow out the candle," she said with a smile.

I was tired of wishing, so I didn't make one. I blew out the candle and forced a smile to let Candice know I appreciated her efforts. I did, but the timing was off. The last thing on my mind was my damn birthday.

Candice sat on the bed and picked up the fork to feed me. I wasn't hungry, so I removed the fork from her hand. "I, uh, really appreciate this, but I kind of want to check out of here for a while and get some sleep."

Candice smiled and placed the tray on the nightstand. She straddled my lap and started to rub my chest. "Lay back, relax, and let me put you to sleep," she offered. "You need all the rest you can get, and I want you to be good and ready for your surprise party tonight. Juan is counting on me to get you there, and I know I shouldn't have told you about it, but I wanted you to be prepared."

I swear the last thing I was up to was partying, but I didn't want to let my niggas down. They knew I had been under a lot of pressure, and I guess they figured this birthday party would do me some good. I couldn't be mad at them for trying to shake me from this slump, so like it or not, I had to show the fuck up at the party and pretend that I didn't know shit about it.

Candice pecked her lips down my bare chest, and she pulled the sheet back to see my dick that was not cooperating. When she touched it with her lips, I pulled on her hair to lift her head. "Sleep," I said. "I want sleep, not head."

Candice moved over in bed next to me and laid her head against my chest. My cell phone rang, and when I looked at the number, it was Mama bugging again. I almost ignored it, but I picked up instead.

"Honey Pooh," she teased. "Stop pouting and step back into the light so I can see my handsome son shine again. I forgot to tell you that your birthday present will arrive within the hour, and all it is is just a little something to show you how much I love and appreciate you. You know I do appreciate you, don't you?"

"Yes, and whatever it is, thank you. Much love to you too, but I need to doze right now, all right?"

"Go 'head and get it in. Trice and I are going to celebrate your birthday by going to the casino tonight. I always get lucky when I play on your birthday. Last year I won almost forty thousand dollars. I'm hoping to double that this year."

"Well, good luck. Tell Trice I said what's up, and I'll get at you later."

I fell asleep after that call, and a few hours later I woke up to a Bugatti parked in my driveway. Mama had definitely outdone herself with this one, but truth be told, material shit didn't really move me that much. She already knew that, but I called to thank her anyway. There was a little more excitement in my voice, and she was happy to hear it.

"Have a good time tonight," she said. "I'll see you soon, and kiss my baby for me when you see her. I was talking about Shania, not Karrine."

"I haven't seen neither of them in about a month, so you gon' have to come to Chicago and give your own kisses."

"Chicago won't see me for a very long time, and shame on Karrine for acting like a damn fool. You really need to do something about this, Honey, and at the end of the day Shania will always be your daughter."

I was already feeling bad because I had expected to hear from Karrine and Shania today. With Mama bringing it up, it upset me. "Karrine is doing what she feels is best, so can we please not talk about this right now?"

"What Karrine is doing is making an ass of herself, and she's denying Shania a chance to be with those who love her. I'm not going to sugarcoat the shit, Honey, and if we don't talk about it today, we will talk about it soon, because Shania needs you. Regardless of what happened, she needs you in her life."

"I get that, but not now. I'm going to take my new ride for a spin and see what this bad boy can do."

Mama laughed and hung up. I wasn't going for a spin right now, but I intended to do so when I got ready for the party tonight.

"Dang, yo' Mama must really, really love you," Candice said as she walked around the car, checking it out.

Mama did love me. Always had. Always would.

Hours later, I stepped out in black-on-black, which turned out to be a crime. My smooth, dark chocolate skin was covered in a black silk button-down shirt from Express Men that was neatly tucked into my black pants. A leather belt matched my shiny leather shoes, and diamonds glistened on my watch, my earring, and my cross necklace that rested against my chest. My shirt was partially unbuttoned, and my light-brown eyes were hidden behind dark, aviator sunglasses. My locs were tied back, but some fell a few inches past my shoulders. After I scented my body with cologne, I headed downstairs to see if Candice was ready to go.

She stood at the bottom of the stairs waiting for me. Her turquoise dress cut across her shoulder, and it was so short that if she lifted her arms the dress would turn into a shirt. Her skin was smooth and chocolate like mine, and her shiny long hair was pulled back into a sleek ponytail that fell all the way to the tip of her butt. Her glittery, peep-toe heels made her damn near as tall as me.

"Well, damn," she said, looking at me. "Yo . . . you look fly as fuck."

"I'ma hit you back with that compliment, but I guess you know that we're already late, right? My phone has been blowing the hell up, and these niggas want me to believe that I'm meeting them to play cards."

Candice smiled. "Yeah, they've been calling me too, wondering where we are. Please don't tell them I told you what was up, and when you walk in there you'd better act surprised."

We left, and I drove the shit out of my new car trying to hurry to the party. I cranked up the music and was doing my best to get hyped. Lil Wayne's lyrics were definitely getting me there, and Future was doing the damn thing, too. By the time I got to our destination, I was high off music. The party was a private event, so I wasn't worried about niggas who I didn't know showing up. This shit was put together by my boys—the ones who had been with me since forever and who I had mad love and respect for.

As planned, Candice led the way. She opened the double doors, and at first there was nothing but darkness. The lights flashed on and everybody there screamed, "Happy Birthday!" I cocked my head back and displayed a smirk on my face as I looked around the crowded room that was thick with my niggas and plenty of bitches. Some of them I knew from the block, some I didn't.

"Awww hell," my boy Melo said. "That nigga knew what was up. I can tell by the look on his face."

Many others agreed, and I tried to convince them that I didn't know. They didn't believe me, so we laughed that shit off and cranked up the music.

In less than an hour, I was feeling this shit. I was high as fuck and was on the dance floor with a slew of bitches surrounding me. The lyrics to the music had me zoned out, and my hands were in the air while one chick was bent over in front of me, another was grinding herself against my backside, one was to my left rubbing my chest, another was raking her fingers through my locs, and I had no idea who was squeezing my steel. The dance floor was jam-packed, and even though I was hot as hell, I continued to dance.

"I want to taste you, Honey," one chick whispered in my ear. I closed my eyes and slowly nodded.

Another chick expressed herself out loudly. "Let's go somewhere and get our fuck on. You know you want this."

I guess she thought I did, especially since she was bent over in front of me, touching her ankles.

"You can have all of us," the one to my left said. "And you ain't leaving here tonight, unless we all are going with you."

I smiled and nodded to the beat of the music. My boys Melo, Juan, Dingo, and Maurice were on the dance floor laughing their asses off. They could tell I was fucked up, and right after the song was over, I managed to stumble away from the chicks, who kept on throwing the pussy at me.

"Take the shades off so I can look into those sexy eyes," one chick said, touching my sunglasses to remove them.

I snatched her wrist and squeezed it. "Don't touch my shit," I said, rejecting her move. "Now back the fuck up."

She moved away from me, and as I smooth walked through the crowd, niggas and bitches parted like the Red Sea. Everybody was calling out for Honey, but I was blazing.

I sat at a reserved table and Candice came up from behind, massaging my shoulders. "Are you ready for your birthday present?" she asked.

I cocked my stiff neck from side to side, appreciating the feel of her hands pressing deep into my shoulders.

"Yeah, I'm ready for it, ma. What you got for me?"

A few minutes later the lights went dim, and as everyone cleared the path in front of me, I looked up and swore that I saw one of the coldest bitches that I had ever seen coming my way. The DJ must have been reading my mind when he had Akon's "I Wanna Fuck U" on repeat. All she had on was a pair of six-inch heels that looked embedded with diamonds. Her caramel skin was dripping with honey, and my eyes scanned in on her shaved pussy hairs that were trimmed into the shape of a butterfly. My niggas were whistling and hollering out all kinds of shit.

"Hit that shit, Honey! Nigga tear that pussy up!"

"We won't be mad if yo' ass want to leave right now!"

"I bet you done sobered the fuck up now nigga!"

Many of the bitches in the room stared with halted breaths as they checked her out. I was speechless my damn self, and the way her body was sculptured made my dick rise to the occasion.

Candice leaned down and whispered in my ear. "I hope you like her. We can take her home with us tonight, and this will be one birthday present that you'll never forget."

When the chick stepped up to me, I lowered my sunglasses down an inch and peered over them. She smiled at me with glee in her sexy-ass eyes, and when she turned around I damn near fell out of my chair. Honey dripped down the curves of her juicy ass, and I swear that if this bitch bent over I was going to have a heart attack.

"You supposed to be lickin' the honey by now!" Melo shouted. "If you won't, every nigga up in here will!"

Everybody looked on, waiting to see what I was going to do. For the moment, that was nothing. She made the next move, and when she attempted to straddle my lap, I held her waist and moved her back.

"Not on my clothes, please. I don't want that honey all over my fit."

While facing me, she bent over and placed the palms of her hands on my knees. The niggas' eyes behind her were locked on her ass, and the looks on their faces said it all. She. Was. One. Bad. Bitch.

"Okay. I won't ruin your clothes, but you must promise me that you'll lick me from head to toe later. I also want to give the birthday boy a kiss, so at least allow me to do that."

I didn't . . . couldn't say shit. I sat there in a trance as she leaned in and brushed her soft lips against mine. Her pierced tongue entered my mouth and she presented me with one of the sweetest tasting kisses I'd ever had. My eyes were closed and I could hear my boys cheering us on. That made me back away from her lips and wipe the wetness from mine.

"Happy birthday," she said in a soft whisper. "Let me know when you're ready to go."

"We will," Candice rushed to say. "And hopefully that'll be soon."

As quickly as the chick came, she went. Candice walked away too, and when several of my niggas came up to me they couldn't stop talking about the bitch. My thoughts were all over the place, but I grabbed Juan around the neck and pulled him to me.

"Did you send out invitations to this party?" I asked.

"Yep. Me and Melo did. Why?"

"Did you send Karrine an invitation?"

"Yep, I did. I thought she would call Leslie to RSVP, but when I checked the list, Karrine's name wasn't on it. I then called her cell phone, but she didn't answer. I left a message for her too, but she didn't hit me back."

I patted Juan on his neck and let it go. I wanted to know if Karrine had known about this party, and obviously she did. I guess she decided not to come, just like I guess she decided not to call and wish me a happy birthday either. That was real fucked up, because over the years, no matter what we had been through or were going through, we always reached out and did special things for each other on our birthdays. I was so sure that I would hear from her today. Deep down, I was real disappointed that I hadn't.

Either way, the party went on. It was off the hook, and as I looked around, everybody seemed to be having a good time. Glasses were being filled with champagne, Kush was being smoked, 'cane was being snorted, and there was free food and drinks for everybody.

For whatever reason, I found myself checking my cell phone every now and then and watching the clock. It was almost midnight, meaning that my birthday would be over and I still hadn't heard from Karrine. Text messages kept coming through, though. Two were from Mama, telling me about her winnings, several were from family, and I even got a text message from Simone who told me to stay away from her sister, but have a good birthday. I let out a chuckle as I read the text message, and sucked in heat from a joint as I sat with some of my boys at the table. Two chicks were standing on top of it dancing, while my niggas made it rain for them. I leaned toward Juan, who sat next to me.

"Man, do me a favor and hit up Karrine on yo' cell phone to see what's up. Maybe she tried to call you back and you didn't answer."

"That ain't the case—and why you keep askin' me about that bitch? If she ain't here, she ain't here."

I glared at Juan and shot him a dirty look that put fear in him. "Nigga, just do what the fuck I said, and pull back on yo' choice of words for my baby's mother. You out of line, and I don't appreciate that shit."

"Look, I'm sorry for sayin' that shit and I apologize. But stop trippin', nigga. Check out all these hoes around here sweatin' you and shit. All I'm sayin' is, be happy and get a vision of what tonight will bring. Yo muthafuckin' bedroom gon' be on fire!"

Juan laughed and patted my back. He checked through his phone and found Karrine's number. After calling it, he listened, then put his cell phone up to my ear. Her voice mail came on.

"Hang up," I said, trying not to show how upset I was. I downed another drink, and when one of the chicks on the table squatted in front of me, I opened my legs and slumped in my seat. The G-string she wore was swallowed by her visible pussy lips. She lifted her finger, motioning for me to come to her. When I didn't move, Juan pulled the G-string away from her pussy lips and slapped a couple hundred dollars between her legs.

"Back up," he said to her. "Chill for a minute."

The chick stood and worked her way down the table. Juan turned to me and sighed. "What's up with you, nigga? Why you actin' all difficult and shit? At first you seemed to be enjoyin' yourself, and now you actin' all fucked up."

I rubbed my hands together, and then stood up to stretch. "I'm good, nigga. Let's go cut the cake. I'm in the mood for cake. You?"

He nodded, then several of my boys followed me as I walked over to another table to cut my cake. Everybody sang "Happy Birthday" to me, and as they sang, my phone vibrated. I hurried to look at my phone, only to see another text from someone else, not Karrine. The time showed 12:47 a.m.—my birthday was officially over.

I got down on some cake, laughed, flirted, and talked shit to my boys for a while. Then I stepped to Juan, who was standing near the dance floor, talking to some chick from the block.

"Ay, cover for me, all right?" I said to him. "I'm about to make a move, and if anybody ask where I went, make up something."

Juan slapped his hand against mine. I thanked him for putting this shit together, and headed toward the back door, hoping that no one would see me exit.

As my hand touched the doorknob, I heard Candice call my name. I turned around, only to see her and the chick from earlier standing in the doorway of a private room. They grinded against each other, and the other chick kept placing delicate kisses on Candice's lips while keeping her eyes on me.

"Where are you going?" Candice asked. "You're not leaving us, are you?"

I put my hands in my pockets and stepped up to them. I was so sure that they could offer me one hell of a night to remember, but I wasn't in the mood for that kind of night. "I appreciate the birthday gift," I said, looking at the other chick, not Candice. "But maybe next time, all right?"

She pouted and batted her lashes. Her eyes were so addictive that I had to look away. "You're welcome," she said. "And Candice has my number, just in case you change your mind."

Without giving it much more thought, I left. I drove at high speeds, trying to get to Karrine's crib so I could confront her about a buildup of bullshit that was on my mind. Rain was coming down so hard that my car kept skidding on my way there. I finally slowed down, after I almost hit a truck on the highway that had abruptly switched lanes. I arrived at Karrine's crib right before three in the morning. I was sure that Shania was sleeping, so I tapped on the door with light, but quick knocks.

"Who the fuck is it?" Karrine said in a grouchy tone that let me know she had been sleeping too.

"Open the door," was all I said.

Karrine opened the door, and when I looked at her, some of my anger subsided. I hadn't seen her since that day at the park, and she looked just as beautiful in a long, pajama shirt with a teddy bear on it. Fuzzy house shoes covered her feet, and most of her hair had been shaved off again.

"What?" she said with attitude.

"Are you gon' let me inside, or do I have to stand out here in the rain and get drenched?"

Karrine stepped outside and closed the door behind her. By being close to the door, she protected herself from the rain, but I was still getting wet.

"I'm not invitin' you inside. Shania is 'sleep and I'm goin' back to bed too."

"You can, once I get in yo' shit about not calling to wish me a happy birthday, and for not showing the fuck up to my surprise party. Why didn't you show up or call to show a nigga some love? You didn't even have Shania call me, and that was some foul shit, Karrine. You know it was, and I know you did that shit on purpose."

She folded her arms and rolled her eyes. "We could care less about yo' damn birthday for real. You fucked hers up by bringin' yo' bitch to the party, so why should we have to break our necks for you on yo' birthday? Nigga please. Get out of here and continue on with 'That Life' and let us live ours."

"I see yo' ass is still bitter about some shit, so I'ma let you go back inside and sleep real tight. You silly, Karrine. Yo' ass is real childish and silly."

I stepped away from the door and into the rain that continued to pour on me. Karrine rushed up from behind me and shoved me in the back. I shot her an angry glare that let her know she needed to back the fuck up.

"Yo' ass the one silly," she hissed. "I've been doin' just fine, until you showed yo' ass up insultin' me and whinin' like a bitch about yo' dumb-ass birthday. Nigga grow up, please!"

I removed my sunglasses and put them in my pocket, just so I could get a good look at her. Something inside of me wanted to knock her on her ass. Something else wanted me to slap the shit out of her or choke the last breath out of her for spewing all this foul shit. I restrained myself from going there, and just stood there, getting drenched and listening to her foolishness.

"We don't need yo' ass," she fussed. "So stop comin' over here and leave us the fuck alone. I expected to hear from your lawyers by now, but I figured Shania didn't mean shit to you anyway, as I surely don't."

I nodded and wiped down my face to clear the raindrops. "That's right. Get it all off yo' chest right now. Have at it, Karrine, and tell me how you really feel. Even if you want to throw punches at me, feel free to do that shit too."

Karrine wasted no time in taking me up on that offer. She slapped the shit out of me and punched me in my chest. Yet again, I nodded. "I see somebody's been brushing up on her fighting skills. But you gon' have to get at me better than that, because those punches at about shit."

She punched me in the chest again, causing me to take one step back. Madness was in her eyes, and she looked devious. "Nigga, you damn right. I have been brushin' up on my fightin' skills, and you ain't never gon' be able to kick my ass like you did at yo' crib that day again! Never, Honey, and I will fight yo' ass again, whenever you're ready for some of this."

I smirked just to piss her off. "So, that's what this is all about? You're still angry about getting yo' ass kicked, huh? Well, let's settle this shit right now. I'm giving you permission to kick my ass right now, but there will be no guarantees that I won't fight back."

Karrine was soaking wet, as I was. Her T-shirt look melted against her body, and I could see that she was wearing nothing underneath. The rain, however, didn't stop her. She punched me in my stomach, and when I bent slightly over to grab it, she smacked me again. I smiled and fought back by planting a soft kiss on her cheek.

"Your turn again," I said. "You're almost there."

She wiped her hand on her cheek, as if she were wiping away my kiss. "Don't put yo' nasty-ass lips on me, fool. Ain't no tellin' how many pussies those lips touched today."

"Plenty," I said, fucking with her.

That made her even madder, so she hit me again. I fought back with another kiss—this time on her lips. She growled and lifted her leg to karate kick me between the legs. I figured she would go there, and I was ready. I grabbed her foot and twisted it.

"Let it go," she shouted.

"Sure."

I let go by pushing her hard and making her fall down on the soggy, wet, and muddy grass. She was really pissed now, and when she charged at me, I shoved her ass down again. Mud was caked on her backside, and as fast as the rain was falling, it still wasn't enough to wash the mud off. I dropped to my knees, feeling my knees sink into the mud.

"Don't touch me," Karrine said. "Back the hell away from me and take yo' ass home."

I started to remove my shirt and pulled it away from my chest. "I will go home, after I get my belated birthday present. You owe me, and I'll be damned if you don't give it to me right now."

Karrine tried to scoot away from me, but all she was doing was covering herself with more mud. "I'm not givin' you shit!" she yelled.

I grabbed her legs and held on to her ankles. I pulled her to me, and held my body up over hers. The diamond cross that hung from my neck rested on her chest as I looked down at her.

"Stop all this madness, ma." I spoke in a soft tone. "Show a nigga some love and quit treating me so ill. I know I've made some mistakes, but that's what humans do. They can change too, and all I ask is that you work with me during the process. I'll get there. I promise."

Karrine searched into my eyes without saying a word. Her chest heaved in and out, making her breasts rise with each breath that she took. As she lay silent, I continued to lay over her. The rain was beating down on my back, and I unbuttoned my pants, then lowered them to my ankles and kicked them off. I felt Karrine's hands ease around my back, and when her legs wrapped around me it felt like something magical was happening. I hurried to slip my dick into her pussy that locked on my steel like this shit was meant to be. I rocked her pussy at a rhythmic pace that made her sweet juices sing out to me.

For the first few minutes, there was silence. All we could hear was the rain beating down on the concrete and the wind whistling. Karrine released her hands from my back and stretched out her arms. She put a high arch in her back, closed her pretty eyes, and squeezed her hands in the mud. Tears rolled from the corners of her eyes and then she opened them to look at me.

"We do need you. I . . . I love you so much that—"

I silenced her words with a kiss. With the mud still in her hands, she reached around me again and rubbed that shit all over my back. It didn't bother me that it felt grimy, because the feel of being inside of her pussy had taken over every feeling in my body. I rolled on my back, and put her on top of me. The pajama shirt she wore was covering what I wanted to see, so I pulled it over her head and tossed it to the side. Karrine worked her pussy well while on top of me, but I wanted to feel her body next to mine. I pulled her to me and she rested her chest against mine. Mud was now in my hands too, so as she sat back up to ride me, I coated her firm breasts and juicy ass with mud. I squeezed in all the right places, and thrust my dick into the depths of her pussy.

"I can't believe we're doin' this," she said in a whisper. "This is such a mess."

"A good mess. And don't act like you're not enjoying it."

Karrine enjoyed it so much that she laid flat on her stomach in the mud. I got behind her, held her hips, and punished her so good from the back that water started to splash as I slapped my wet body against hers. My dick was throbbing so fast inside of her gushy folds. I felt the explosion that was about to take place, and it wasn't long before my hot lava sprayed into her pussy like a water hose. I was so relieved that I dropped my limp body on top of hers. I released several deep breaths, and then placed a trail of soft kisses along the side of her neck.

"To hell with that Bugatti," I said. "This shit right here was waaaay better than that muthafucka."

Karrine lifted her head and looked up at the sky. The rain had slowed, and there was now a whole lot of mud caked on our bodies. "A car will never satisfy you like I can, so let's go inside to wash this off. Then I'll be able to give you your real birthday present. Believe it or not, I did get you one."

"Whatever it is, take it back to where you got it from. I just got what I wanted, and it's all I needed right now."

Karrine pursed her lips. "Nigga, is that all you wanted—some pussy?"

"Nah, not pussy. What I got was a reality check. Thanks for giving it to me."

Karrine smiled and we got up. Our bodies were so stiff, and we laughed as we went inside and left a trail of mud on the floors. We checked on Shania, who was still asleep, and then Karrine joined me in the shower, where she spent the next several hours honoring my birthday wishes and making up for lost time.

## *Karrine*

## 12

Honey left around three in the afternoon, promising me that whenever he came back, things would be different. I didn't care if that was one week from now, one month or one year . . . things had to be different, and he knew exactly what he had to do.

For now, I was riding high off last night. I had been so miserable, and my life just didn't seem right without him. But after all that had happened, I had to fall far back and not reach out to him for anything. I didn't want to keep Shania away from him, but I had to. What had happened that day at the park sent off signals that let me know how quickly Shania could be taken away from us. Honey had put himself in plenty of bad situations, and he now had to take the time to correct some things.

During that time, I told him that I wasn't going to pressure him, and I wasn't going to make any demands. I wasn't going to keep ringing his phone, nor was I going to pay him any visits. Shania and I were staying right here, and at this point, whatever was going to be, would be.

Simone was on her way to come get me so we could go see Chyna. I missed my big sis so much, and I talked to her as often as I could. I had been to see her several times before, and all I could say was that she was hanging in there.

Chyna was the toughest one of all, and I think that Mama's genes ran deeper in her, more than they did in me or Simone. Chyna had made some bad choices that had caught up with her and cost her dearly. But she was also a fighter who I believed would pull through these tough times.

When Simone pulled up in her car, I was coming from my neighbor's house where I had dropped Shania off. My neighbor was a sweet lady in her fifties who had latched on to Shania the day I moved in. She had a grandbaby who was a year older than Shania, and the two of them played well together. I felt comfortable leaving Shania with her, but since the incident at the park, it was rare that Shania would be with anyone else, other than me.

As for Mama, I hadn't spoken to her. It wasn't that I was mad at her or anything like that, the problem was that she was still upset with me. She felt as if had taken Shania away from her, and that I was trying to take Honey away from her too. That was not the case, but she made it out to be like that.

I got in the car and reached over to give Simone a hug.

"What's up, Miss Fashionista?" I said to Simone, because no matter where she went, she was always rocking high-priced shit that looked good on her.

"Nothing much, but the question is what's up with you and all this giddiness? You got that big, bright smile on your face, and I guess it may have somethin' to do with Honey's birthday bein' yesterday."

Simone drove off, and I just kept on smiling. She shoved my shoulder, begging me to tell her the reason for my demeanor. I broke every detail down to her, and shared with her what I wanted Honey to do going forward.

"That mud sex shit sounds nasty, but it also sounds like somethin' me and the professor may wanna try. I bet if we put that shit in front of the screen, mofo's would pay big dollars to see us."

"So you and him still gettin' down like that, huh?"

"Almost every day, with the exception of the weekend. And don't judge me, either, Karrine, because I'm doin' what I need to do right now to get some for-real paper. I'm still in school too, but right now I'm gettin' my master's degree in pimpin' niggas for they money. Since I added the professor to the mix, I have even more clients. They get a kick out of us gettin' our fuck on, but then there are those who still prefer to see me all by my lonesome self."

"Listen, I'm not judgin' you at all. Your life seems to be waaay better than me and Chyna's put together, and I don't suspect that a lot of drama is involved in what you're doin'."

"I'm drama-free, nigga-free, and Mama-free. Things couldn't be better, and I talk to that crazy lady almost every day. She's real hurt by not bein' able to spend time with her gangsta baby, but I told Mama that she was too attached. With you bein' in Chicago, you can do your own thing and get yo' life back on track. Livin' with Mama wasn't a good thing, and the key is to stop dependin' on her so much."

I high-fived Simone. "I ditto that shit, and must agree with what you said. One day at a time, though, baby sis. One day at a fuckin' time."

I gazed out of the window, thinking about Honey. I wondered what he was doing and what he was thinking. I hoped that I wasn't wrong about what I suspected he would do, and if I was, I knew that it was going to affect me in a way that was major.

Simone started telling me about how Mama was kicking Chyna out while she was in jail. It wasn't determined yet where Chyna would have to do her ten-year bid at, but she was now at a facility that only housed a few hundred prisoners. There was no question that she would be transferred soon, and according to Simone, Mama was doing her best to make sure Chyna had everything she needed.

"That's Mama for you," I said. "I'm sure she would do the same for any of us, but I'ma do my very best to make sure jail and me never have anything in common."

"Same here," Simone said. "I'm done with a lot of the unnecessary bullshit, too. This shit with Chyna opened my eyes. I went home and got rid of all my damn guns, and you won't ever hear about me shootin' nobody again."

"Bitch, please. Yo' ass need to quit lyin'. I bet you a thousand dollars that if I go to your place right now, I'll find at least two or three guns."

We laughed, knowing that what Simone had said was a bunch of bull. If need be, we would always turn to our guns for backup.

About three hours later, Simone, Chyna, and me sat at a table laughing and talking about things that were transpiring in our lives. It was hard on me to see Chyna like this, and I could tell that she was putting up a front for us. Her baggy clothes looked nothing like the bad-ass clothes she rocked when we were all together, and her hair was now without braids. It had grown way past her shoulders, and was parted through the middle, nappy as fuck. We teased her about that shit, too, but she always laughed it off.

"Damn, do y'all bitches think I should be rocking Prada up in here or something? And it ain't as if I can reach over and grab a relaxer and style my fuckin' hair. Accept me as is, and when y'all get done talkin', I still look better than both of y'all bitches."

We laughed and highly disagreed. As the conversation went on, Chyna mentioned something that caught me off guard.

"What you mean that Desmon has disappeared?" I questioned.

Chyna gave me a funny look and she smirked. "Have you spoken to Honey lately?"

I nodded, but wasn't sure where she was going with this. "Yeah, I have, but what does he—"

My stomach tightened when Simone asked if she needed to spell it out for me. I didn't say another word, and right then, I knew that Honey had done something to Desmon, probably per Mama's request. I'd thought about calling him to find out, but I meant what I'd said about allowing him time to correct all that was going on with him.

Like always, when it was time to leave Chyna, my eyes watered. Simone and Chyna were never as emotional as I was, but I'm sure that Chyna understood how difficult this was for me too. We gave our good-byes, and as Simone and me left, I walked away thinking that I couldn't wait until the day came when my big sis would be set free. She definitely deserved better than this bullshit.

# HONEY

## 13

The celebration had been over with for about two weeks now, and I was ready to make some moves that needed to be made. Mama and I were supposed to meet with some Mexicans about a major deal they wanted to swing our way, but I had been feeling real uneasy about it. While the deal was worth millions, whenever my gut told me something wasn't right, I tried to listen.

Besides that, I wasn't feeling none of this shit anymore. The day of reckoning had arrived, and like it or not, I was prepared to spill my guts to Mama. There was no doubt that I was making this move because of Karrine, but I was also doing it for myself. Some niggas did it just to make the bitches in their lives happy, but I was doing it because I was tired of living like this. I was sick of Mama depending on me so much, and my baby girl needed a daddy that was smart enough not to put her life at risk. Shit happened, no matter what, but it didn't make sense for me to continue on the path I was traveling.

When I arrived at Mama's house, she was chilling by the poolside with a wide-brim hat on that shielded her face from the bright sun. Sunglasses covered her eyes, and a fishnet wrap covered part of the one piece swimming suit she wore. Several drinks with umbrellas in them sat next to her, and she had a book in her hand. I walked up and sat down in the lounging chair next to her.

"What's that you're reading?"

"I don't know what the title of this book is, but this damn author got my head over here spinning. There's too much bullshit going on, but I must say that I'm loving the drama this nigga cooked up."

Mama laid the book on her lap and removed the hat from her head. She fanned herself with it, then tossed it like a flying saucer into the blue water.

"You're early," she said. "I thought you weren't coming here until tomorrow."

"I wasn't, but I'm here today because I'm turning in my resignation. I need to pull back from this shit and be done with it. I'm well aware that I made some serious promises to you over the years, but I just can't do this shit anymore. I'm stressed the fuck out, and this shit ain't fun like it used to be."

Mama looked at me without a blink. She sucked in a deep breath then released it. "So, is this really Honey talking to me, or are you Karrine in disguise?"

"Don't go there with this. This is more about me wanting to do something different than it is about anything else."

"Something different like what? Work at a fast-food restaurant, wash some cars or become a bellhop? Honey, please. Get out of my face with this mess. We've come too far together, and there will be no turning back. I expect for you to pick me up tomorrow about eight in the evening. If you're not here, you know what happens."

Mama lifted her glass and sipped from the red straw. I didn't expect for this to be easy, and I put forth every effort not to disrespect her.

"Unfortunately, I'm gon' have to turn back, and it's yo' choice if you want to proceed. I don't know what occupation to pursue, but you are speaking to a nigga with a college degree, who may have some options. What

I expect is for you to respect my wishes, salute me for all that I've done, and make peace with this situation so that we can continue on loving each other as mother and son."

Mama sat up and saluted me. "You can take that college degree that I paid for and shove it clean up yo' ass. Nigga, I am in disbelief that you have allowed a piece of pussy to come between what we built together. You gon' let that shit destroy everything, and you know damn well, Honey, that you were made for this shit. It's in yo' blood, nigga, it's in yo' blood! You will never be satisfied playing house with Karrine, and if you think that I'm going to make contributions to muthafuckas who continue to stab me in my back, you are sadly mistaken. If you walk, you walk as a broke nigga. I want all of my shit back, and there is no damn way that I'm going to reward you for walking out at a time like this!" Mama pounded her leg with her fist and shook her head. "I can't believe I got this deal going down tomorrow, and you're out here talking crazy!"

I wasn't down with her tone, so I snapped. "Jus . . . just get somebody else to do it! You act like can't nobody else do this shit, and I know several niggas right now who would love to take my damn place and deal with yo' shit!"

Mama looked like she wanted to slap the hell out of me, but when she lifted her hand, all she did was squeeze her fist. "I don't trust those muthafuckers, and I told Fernando and Luis that they would meet you. They want to meet you, and they do not trust no one else! I would look like a fool if I have to tell them somebody else is coming, and they may call this shit off!"

I shook my head. "Sorry. I can't do it, Mama, and I honestly do not feel right about meeting with those niggas. I heard some bad shit about them, and while you may trust them, I don't."

Mama's jaw dropped. "I've heard some bad shit about you, too. Tell me what that means, and when

did you start doing business dealings with church folk
only? I . . . I just don't know what else to say to you,
Honey, but I will say that I am highly disappointed.
All that loyalty talk was a bunch of bull, and I never
expected for you to do me like this."

Mama was putting on the guilt trip, but I wasn't buying
it. I stood and looked up at Trice staring out of the huge
picture window from afar. I figured that Mama would go
to her to handle the business now, only because she was
the only other person who Mama trusted.

"I hoped that you would understand this, but I figured
that you wouldn't. When the dust settles, you know
where and how to reach me."

"When the dust settles, I hope you rot in hell. My hope
is that you fall flat on yo' face and have to come crawling
back to me. Then I will spit in your face and send you
running back home to that heifer Karrine, who has no
clue what you're made of. I told you to never bite the
hand that feeds you, but my hand has now been chewed
off, and my business will be left on life support until I can
figure out what to do. Thank you, Honey, for fucking me
over! Now, get the hell off my property before I splatter
your goddamn brains all over the place, you punk-ass
nigga!"

It took a lot out of me to walk away from Mama, but
I did, not knowing if I would catch a bullet in my back
today or on the days following. Mama being this mad
was never a good thing, and there was always a price to
pay when she felt betrayed. It wasn't wise to fuck up her
paper either, and I knew the risk I was taking for cutting
this shit short.

For the next few days, I stayed in California. I wanted
to see what kind of damage Mama would do, and it
appeared that she was really trying to shut me down and
put me out of commission for good. I couldn't say that I

didn't expect this, but my name had been removed from all of the bank accounts, the house no longer belonged to me, my cars had been taken away, and my phones had been disconnected. Some of the friends I had, I had no more, and Mama already had them on her team. The word was that Mama's deal turned out to be a huge success. By sending Trice, she wounded up negotiating more than what was originally agreed upon, but two niggas on Mama's team were shot dead during negotiations because one of the Mexicans thought he'd had beef with them before.

It was that kind of shit that made me nervous. The money was good, no doubt, but there were so many risks. Risks that I didn't want to take anymore, although many did pay off. Like the one I took by being in charge of the books. Mama didn't actually think that she could leave me high and dry or broke as shit, did she? I knew she was smarter than that, and so was I. So smart that over the years, I had stashed enough money aside for rainy days. I knew this day would come, and even though I hadn't put aside enough to keep the same lifestyle flowing, I did put aside enough. Enough for me, for my woman, and for my baby to live on comfortably.

I left Cali feeling so-so. There was a delay with my plane, but within several hours I was back in Chicago. Without any further delays, I rented a car and drove it straight to Karrine's crib. When she opened the door, all we did was stare at each other. I then cracked a tiny smile, one that let her know that everything was final. She threw her arms around my neck, expressing her enthusiasm for the one she now recognized as a changed man. A nigga could do that shit if he wanted to, but it took the right kind of chick to elevate him to the next level in life. As for now, the shit felt good.

# Epilogue

## *Karrine*

Eight months later, our wedding day had finally arrived. Honey and I stood in front of a Justice of the Peace, confessing our love for each other at the courthouse. The only person that we had invited to come was Mama. In our hearts, we truly wanted closure with her crazy self, but by the time the ceremony was over, it was obvious that we wouldn't get it.

At least we tried. Honey couldn't be mad at himself about that, and neither could I. Our relationship had changed in so many ways, but there were a few times when Honey would speak about how much he missed having so much power, and about the many millions that he'd made. I realized that he was still a work in progress, as we all were. But the one thing that I was sure of was that he would never go back to "That Life." The life that gave him wealth, but delivered so much pain. It almost caused him to lose out on everything, and he just didn't want that for himself. Some niggas did. Including Mama, who was the real *Money-Makin' Mama* in all of this. She would maintain her status until the day she died, but by then I hoped that we would one day settle our differences.

Honey and I sat in the car kissing each other as if the world was ending today. He looked so handsome in his black suit, and the white, baby-doll dress I wore was fit for the occasion. I scooted over to sit as close as I could to him, and right after he started the car, we saw a fat black dude rushing our way. Honey squinted and quickly reached underneath the seat to retrieve his Glock. We both panicked, but I thought the nigga looked familiar. As he smiled at me and Honey and walked up to the car, Honey lowered the window. His finger was on the trigger, and I was sure that the fat dude saw the gun in Honey's hand.

"Easy," he said to Honey with his hands open so we could see them. "All I came to do was give you this, compliments of yo' Mama."

We didn't know what the hell the nigga had reached into his jacket to get, but Honey lifted the gun and aimed it, ready to shoot.

The dude pulled out a card and carefully eased it through the slightly lowered window. "Have a good day," he said to us. "Congrats."

The card dropped inside of the car, and the dude backed away with his hands still in the air. After he disappeared, Honey laid the gun on his lap and held the card in his hand.

"Can a bomb fit in here?" he asked, then moved his ear close to the card. We laughed.

"No, but that ricin and anthrax shit can. Open it slowly and be careful."

We laughed again as Honey opened the card. It was a beautiful wedding card, congratulating us on our special day. Mama had written something special, and there was a five-dollar bill inside:

*Tell that bitch Karrine that she'd better take good care of you, and nigga you'd better do your*

*damnedest to see about her ass, too! Give gangsta baby a huge kiss for me, and I will see her when she turns sixteen. By then, I'm sure she'll need someone for-real guidance. As for the five dollars, take yo' wife to McDonalds and buy yourself a Big-fucking-Mac! I'm sure it's all y'all broke asses can afford right now, but nonetheless, there is still some love left in my heart. Not much, so maybe I'll see y'all in about fifteen years, or when Chyna gets out. Until then, stay the fuck away from me, and don't bother to call and thank me, please!*
   *Mama*

We cracked up. Honey tucked the five dollars in his pocket, and pulled the car away from the curb. When I asked where we were going, he was seriously on his way to McDonald's.

"Nigga, please. You'd better take me somewhere extravagant and wine and dine me all night. McDonald's ain't gon' work, and you'll be in there eatin' that Big Mac all by yourself."

"If I can't take you to McDonalds, then I'm going to take you to a hotel room right now and fuck you until my dick falls off. You won't be eating shit, because I'ma wear that ass—"

My body quivered, and I welcomed his bright idea. "Stop talkin', nigga, and speed it up, then. Unless you want to pull the car over, again, and give me a quick tease of what I can expect."

Honey swerved the car over to the side and turned to me. I could tell something was on his mind, and of course it was Mama. "Don't know love or show love, unless it's for the love of family," he said. "I guess that shit really does apply, and I hope you appreciate all this brotherly love I've been giving you."

I pursed my lips and teased him. "I guess. It's been a'ight, and you need to step up yo' game, cause I know some niggas whose head game be on fire! On a scale from one to ten, I give you about a two!"

Honey let out a cackling, wicked laugh and made me eat my words when he raised my dress and dropped low into my lap. My eyes fluttered, and I gasped to catch my breath so I could express my thoughts to the one who made my life worth living. My ten-star nigga, Honey.